*Peirene*

*VÉRONIQUE OLMI*

*TRANSLATED FROM THE FRENCH
BY ADRIANA HUNTER*

# Bord
# de
# Mer

AUTHOR

Véronique Olmi, born in 1962 in Nice, is a highly acclaimed French dramatist and her twelve plays have won numerous awards. *Bord de Mer*, published in 2001 in France, was her first novel and has become an international bestseller. Her seventh novel came out in 2010.

TRANSLATOR

Adriana Hunter has translated over 50 books from French, including works by Agnès Desarthe, Véronique Ovaldé and Hervé Le Tellier. She won the 2011 Scott Moncrieff Prize for her translation of *Beside the Sea*, and has been short-listed twice for the Independent Foreign Fiction Prize.

MEIKE ZIERVOGEL
PEIRENE PRESS

This is the most impressive novel about the mother and child relationship I have read. Véronique Olmi handles an aspect of motherhood that we all too often deny. She depicts a woman's fear of releasing her children into the world. The simple first person narrative achieves an extraordinary level of poetry and inner truth.

First published in Great Britain in 2010 by
Peirene Press Ltd
17 Cheverton Road
London N19 3BB
www.peirenepress.com

Reprinted February 2010, May 2012

Originally published in French as
BORD DE MER
Copyright © Véronique Olmi / Actes Sud, 2001

English Translation Copyright © Adriana Hunter, 2010

This book is supported by the French Ministry of Foreign Affairs, as
part of the Burgess programme run by the Cultural Department of the
French Embassy in London. (www.frenchbooknews.com).

Liberté • Égalité • Fraternité
RÉPUBLIQUE FRANÇAISE

ISBN 978-0-9562840-2-0

Designed by Sacha Davison Lunt
Photographic image: Irene Nam / Flickr / Getty Images
Printed and bound by T J International, Padstow, Cornwall

VÉRONIQUE OLMI

TRANSLATED FROM THE FRENCH
BY ADRIANA HUNTER

*Peirene*

# Beside
# the
# Sea

For Douchka

We took the bus, the last bus of the evening, so no one would see us. The boys had their tea before we left, I noticed they didn't finish the jar of jam and I thought of that jam left there for nothing, it was a shame, but I'd taught them not to waste stuff and to think of the next day.

Leaving on the bus I think they were happy, a bit anxious, too, because I hadn't explained anything. I'd brought their jackets in case it rained, it often rains by the sea – that I had told them, at least, they were going to see the sea.

It was Kevin, the little one, who seemed happiest, more inquisitive anyway. But Stan kept giving me suspicious looks like when I just sit in the kitchen and he watches me, thinking I don't know he's there, barefoot, in his pyjamas, I don't even have the strength to say Don't stay there with nothing on your feet, Stan. Yes, sometimes I sit in the kitchen for hours and I couldn't give a stuff about anything.

Luckily, we didn't have to wait long for the bus and no one saw us leave. It felt really strange driving away from the city, leaving it for this unknown place, specially as it wasn't the holidays and that's what the boys kept thinking, I know they did. We'd never been away for a holiday, never left the city, and suddenly life felt new, my stomach was in knots, I was thirsty the whole time and everything was irritating, but I did my best, yes really my best, so the kids didn't notice anything. I wanted us to set off totally believing in it.

When the bus turned up we all felt nervous, shy like. We couldn't have felt more uncomfortable going into a luxury cabin on a first-class cruise ship. It was only a noisy old bus with no heating, mind you. Oh yes, it was certainly cold. You got into the thing and it felt like walking into a draught.

I paid our fares with the last big banknote I had, and we went and sat at the back, the boys and me, with our sports bags at our feet, I'd stuffed them full of warm clothes for the kids, there were too many clothes, I know, but it was quite a panic packing those bags, I can't explain it. I wanted to put everything into them, I knew it was pointless, I wanted it to come with us, stuff from home, familiar things, things you recognize as yours straight away. Kevin wanted me to take his toys, too, but I didn't want to, I knew pretty well we wouldn't be playing.

There were a lot of people around us, unbelievable that there are so many people out there, specially so late, where were they all from, were they going to the same place as us, no way of knowing, they looked calm, lost in quiet thoughts. My kids were full of questions, Is it going to take long? Will it be light when we get there? Things like that, I wasn't sure what to tell them, I felt sick and didn't really want to talk, I definitely didn't want to give other people a chance to listen to us.

We were high up in the bus, so cars – which are normally so frightening – were pathetic little contraptions now, we could see the drivers' hands, their legs, their stuff on the passenger seat, see them almost as clearly as if they'd been sitting in their own homes, it made them seem less dangerous, yes, we felt better protected in that bus, even if we were dying of cold.

It wasn't long before Kevin needed a wee. It's just nerves, I told him, but he started to worry, he was afraid he'd do it in his pants, he's easily worried. And me who didn't want to attract attention, I had to go down the aisle in front of everyone, to stop the bus and have my boy pee against the wheel, in the dark, by the side of the road, cars whooshing past with a fierce flash of headlights. Stan, now he's never a problem. Never a pee. Never hungry. Nor thirsty. He never asks for anything, sometimes it bothers me a bit, I'd prefer it if he'd look at me less and whinge a bit more. Now it doesn't matter any longer.

Stan was like the older brother even before Kevin was born. It was like that was just what he was waiting for: for the littl'un to come along so that he could take on the role of big brother. It really suits him. In the morning, I don't have the strength to get up to go to school, it's Stan who takes Kevin, and I think the littl'un likes it. With Stan I'm never late, he told me once. Schools open too early. Ten o'clock would be good. I can't do anything before ten o'clock. I don't sleep well at night. It's the worrying. I couldn't tell you what about. It's like something's been lowered onto me... like someone sitting on me, that's it. No one even notices I'm here. They sit down on me like sitting on a bench. I'd like to get up, stand up, thrash and scream. Nothing doing. They keep on sitting there. How can anyone understand that? I'm being smothered at night. That's why I often have to lie down in the daytime. To sleep a bit. In the daytime I can sleep without worrying. Not always, but it does sometimes work, a transparent sleep, a pause which leaves no memories afterwards, and no pain either. When I wake up it's hard – I don't even know where I am. What time it is. What I'm supposed to be doing. I often miss the end of school. I feel ashamed and rush off to the school, and Kevin's waiting by the gate, crying. He's always frightened, not for himself, for me. I'm not that fragile... but I am ashamed.

The bus journey was long, too long, it was dark, we couldn't see the countryside so we didn't know where we were or where we were going. There we sat in the darkness, in the noise, driving past lights, overtaking lorries, overtaking but to go where exactly?

The windows were all misted up, Kevin made pictures with his finger, lopsided little houses, people without arms – Kevin always draws people without arms, They've got their hands behind their backs, that's what he says when you ask him where their arms have gone.

It wasn't long before there was no room left to draw on the window and Kevin got bored, he asked for his noonoo, he wanted to sleep, I'd completely forgotten the noonoo. Stan gave me a dirty look, He'll just have to suck his thumb, I said, children never used to have noonoos, they sucked their thumbs, it was much simpler. I said that but I knew Kevin couldn't get to sleep without his big yellow hanky. His lips started to quiver. Don't cry, Kevin! said Stan, knowing how tears get started. My noonoo! the littl'un said. Suck your thumb, I said. He kicked the seat in front, the man turned round, a great tall man with a moustache, Kevin was terrified when he told him to stop straight away, and he stopped straight away. He didn't ask for his noonoo any more, I think he was crying, he kept sniffing, it was irritating.

The people in that bus were really settled and comfortable, and they didn't want to be disturbed, that was obvious. They didn't look out at the road but chatted a bit, very quietly. My kids were the only ones who were so wound up, talking loudly, peeing and blubbing. The others, you could tell, all felt safe and sound, you'd have thought they made this trip every evening. There was me losing track of where we were or how long it was since we left, and they just got more and more patient, some of them even slept, hands on their stomachs, mouths open, they knew the journey better than anyone, I was so afraid of missing the stop that I got up again to ask the driver.

I almost fell over in the aisle, the bus was taking a nasty corner and I bumped an old lady's head, she gave an exasperated little cry like I'd been bugging her right from the start, a little cry without even looking at me, maybe she thought I was disgusting. Still, it was good I asked, it was only another ten minutes or so, and the driver said he'd call out the stop, I think he realized I was worried. I thanked him a lot, I was so relieved! I went back to my seat very quietly, holding the backrests firmly, the old woman didn't deign to look at me, she was talking to the man next to her, maybe about me.

We're nearly there, I told the boys and, even though he was crying, Kevin gave me a little smile, one of his little dimple smiles, that's what I call them, with his three missing teeth – we're the same at last, the two of us, with the gaps in our gums. Quite often I daren't smile or laugh without putting my hand over my mouth, I don't know whether Stan and Kevin have noticed. Later they'd have been ashamed, bound to be. Now that we knew where we were we could pretend we didn't give a damn about anything, didn't feel any danger, like the other passengers. It made the time go faster and we were surprised when the driver talked into his mike to say the name of the town. We got up quick, the aisle was full of people.

I was right to bring things for the rain, we took such a dousing when we got off the bus! It's raining from the lights, Kevin said, Stan made fun of him but I thought it was sweet, It's raining from the street lights, you're right, Kevin, I said, roll on morning! I was completely exhausted, plonked I had no idea where in this unknown town, but I acted like I knew my way and followed the people who got off the bus with us, you'd have thought they were all going to the same place, no one hesitating. The boys clung to me, one on each hand, dragging their sports bags with their free hands, they were too heavy for them but ever since I broke my collar bone I've had trouble carrying stuff.

It must have been raining for a long time in that town, it felt more like walking across a building site than along a pavement, unless the place just didn't have pavements. I wondered whether the hotel would let us in with our muddy shoes, and how did people manage here, their houses must be full of water and mud, not to mention sand from the sea. Yes, the sea, obviously we couldn't see it but we couldn't hear it either, my head started hurting really badly when I thought I might have made a mistake, and how was I going to cope in this town full of water and mud if there was no sea, because I'd promised myself my boys would get to see the sea for once in their lives. That was just the way it was. It had to be.

We came to a square and people went off in their different directions, we must have been in the middle of the town, was it huge or tiny, I couldn't make it out, it was so dark, the rain was so cold, we felt like we were in the middle of nowhere, I was almost alone with my kids and the town became a mystery. I didn't know which road to take, where to cross, what would take us away and what would bring us closer, nothing moved and the quieter it became the more out of place we felt.

I had to talk to someone. I don't like asking for help, but it would soon be the middle of the night and then the three of us really would be abandoned. I saw a little man on a street corner, he was huddled into his anorak and walking a dog so flipping small and thin it could have been made of matchsticks – I asked him where the hotel was. My voice was shaky and had trouble getting out, Here come the worries again, I thought and it frightened me. The little man didn't open his mouth, he pointed: the hotel was right behind us, I hadn't seen it, right behind us, but there wasn't a sign lit up, not even a light in the doorway, I thanked him with a quick nod, I was afraid of hearing my own voice and anyway he wasn't opening his mouth either. When we set off again, dragging our bags in the mud, the little matchstick dog started barking, and it sounded like laughter, spiteful laughter, and that sent shivers down my spine – it's not like I'm afraid of dogs or anything, and I could have crushed that one with my hand. I suddenly thought it might have been because of the rain: my voice shaking, the dog laughing, maybe everyone was hoarse in this town and that made it terrifying, I couldn't wait for it to be morning so I could see it all in daylight and check exactly where the horizon took us.

Is this the hotel, Mum? Kevin asked, and *his* voice was packing in, too, but this was his over-tired voice, I knew it so well it was almost reassuring. Go in, I said, and we had to let go of each other, we wouldn't fit through the door holding on to each other like that, not to mention the sports bags. It was hard letting go, our arms were numb and all tangled up, and Kevin got his feet caught in the straps of his bag, his head thudded into the door, that's when I saw how wet his hair was and I remember — it's stupid — I remember, it was like a reflex, an age-old fear, I was afraid he'd catch cold. Get a fever. Who knows? Perhaps all mothers do it: protecting their children from fevers, maybe it's an animal thing, it's stronger than us.

Stan took the two sports bags and he said After you, Mum, he loves it, Stan does, being polite, I'm not used to it myself, I sometimes wonder how come the boy's got such nice manners, where did he learn that? Not at home, that's for sure, and even less at school which is such a tough place. He's polite, yes, but he's strong. That's what's so nice. Having both together. How many times have they tried to bully him into giving up his money at school? Well, he's never given in, he's always fought, even if it cost him hours of detention and punishments, he's always defended himself so fiercely, I don't know where he gets it from. Yes, with me Stan's a real gentleman, he's the only boy who treats me so nicely, it makes me laugh sometimes, of course, I tell him, Stan, stop putting on airs, but I love it and I think he knows it.

In the end we managed to get into the blinking hotel, all numb and wet as we were. It was very dark, there was a tiny night light on the counter and everything was brown: the walls, the lino, the doors, it was an old-fashioned brown – they can't have repainted the place for centuries, and it looked like years of dirt had stuck to the walls and floor, it was like being inside a cardboard box, a shoe box actually.

I could see the boys were disappointed, it's true that on the telly hotels don't look like that, there are lights, flowers, big mirrors, red carpets and people dressed like they're going to a wedding. Behind the counter there was a youngish bloke watching a titchy black-and-white TV, it looked like a security monitor but he was watching a football match, he hardly even looked up when I said my name, he just reached his arm behind him and unhooked a big key which he put down on the counter, mumbling Sixth floor third door left. I was quite glad he wasn't that interested in us, we'd put mud everywhere and you could even see it on the brown lino, it was in little piles, a scatter of poos. I took the key and started looking round, the bloke must have been used to it, The stairs're behind you, he muttered. Well, I definitely was disorientated in this place, everything was always behind me and I didn't know it, everything was there, and I just kept turning, turning round and round while everything waited for me.

It wasn't the stairs I was looking for, it was the lift, but, well, we were nearly there, that's what mattered. Come on, boys, I said, one last effort, and Stan took Kevin's bag, the littl'un took my hand and he said Is this the hotel? again. You're going to have a lovely bed with brand-new sheets, I said, but it didn't cheer him up, I haven't got my noonoo, you forgot my noonoo! His voice was full of resentment, I'm sure he hadn't pictured our little trip like this. Wait till tomorrow when he sees the sea! I thought. I couldn't see how that — the sea — could disappoint us, it's the same everywhere for everyone and I was perfectly capable of taking my kids to see it, thank you very much, I could travel at night, it's not true that I'm paralyzed by my anxieties, like they say at the health centre.

I mulled all this over as we climbed up the stairs, but I didn't really believe it, it was just to get my nerve up. Deep down I couldn't wait to get it over with. But I also knew that the boys had to see the sea, and the thought of all this time to ourselves made my head spin, I hung on to the banister and it felt like it was pulling me, pulling me by my arm. Stan was having trouble with the sports bags, he wanted to stop on the fourth floor. Oh, no! I said, if we stop we'll never start again! I let go of Kevin's hand to help Stan carry one of the bags, hard to say who was helping who, who was hanging on to what, one thing was sure: we were pretty depressed about having to climb so many floors, the staircase was steep and there was no light, perhaps if there'd been a light we'd have felt more like it. Without light it was like going into a tunnel, an underpass, we couldn't picture what the room was going to be like, everything was too brown, too dark, no space for the imagination.

Kevin was jealous because he was tagging along behind, because I was helping his brother, I'm sure of that, and he started to cry, saying he was tired and even saying he wanted to go home! Well, that knocked the stuffing out of me! What? I said, Mum pays for you to go to the seaside and you want to go home? There's school tomorrow, what are we going to tell Marie-Hélène? We'll take her back a seashell, I replied, and I thought perhaps we should do that, choose a seashell and give it to the teacher, my son's first love, yes, give her his first seashell. Now that made Kevin smile, and I was proud of myself, I know how to handle my kids, I thought, I just need to be left to get on with it, would a social worker have thought of that? Getting a five-year-old to climb six floors by talking about seashells? Of course she wouldn't have thought of it, it wasn't even in her questionnaires. "Do you talk to your children about seashells: every day, once a year, never." Well, I'll bet there are plenty who'd say Never, and yet they'd be the ones who call themselves good mothers, just because instead of getting to school at six o'clock they pitch up with their chocolate biscuits at twenty-five past four and grab their children, moaning You were the last one out. Huh! What matters more when it all comes down to it? Seashells, of course, and I was determined to find a really big one, one of those ones that rumble when you put them up to your ear, and look pretty on a sideboard.

It worked a treat, with the whole seashell thing we got to the sixth floor like a dream, me, the kids and the bags. We didn't have any mud left on our shoes, we were sweating, exhausted and boiling hot, ready to go to bed, and I felt a moment of happiness. I just wanted the kids to go straight to bed so that, easy as you please, we'd suddenly find it was the next morning, like other people do, the ones who go to bed at night because they're tired, because they've managed to fill every hour of their day, and they get up in the morning because it's normal, it has to be done and they do it – not like me who gets day and night all confused, who sits up while everyone else is crashed out and collapses when they're all prancing around, and whenever I go out I wonder where everyone's going, charging in every direction, tramping up and down the streets, some of them even make phone calls while they walk, how can anyone be that busy?

I put the big key into the lock of the third door on the left, that's what the nightwatchman had said, and I hadn't got it wrong, third on the left, the door opened... well, not all the way because it knocked into the bed which took up the whole room. We slipped inside and all three of us sat down on it, there wasn't anything else to do, there was no table, no chair, no wardrobe, nope, just the bed, and the room was hardly bigger than that bed.

I was worried Kevin would ask Is this the hotel? again, so I quickly told him Kevin, wee-wee then bed! Where? he asked. Where what? Wee-wee. I put out my hand to open the door and sidled out into the corridor, Kevin followed me, looking very unsure. The light was flickering like the bulb was about to blow, but it didn't. I went along the corridor, it was full of numbered doors and at the end there were two grey doors which said "WC" and "Shower". Phew! I'd been worried we might have to go back down to the first floor and I wouldn't have had the heart to do it, no, I'd rather have had my kid pee out the window. That was when I realized the hotel was deserted, we hadn't met anyone and, apart from the bulb on the blink, we couldn't hear anything.

I opened the door to the toilet and pointed at it to Kevin, it stank in there, it really did, it smelt of sewers and rust, and the flush was dripping onto the toilet seat. Kevin didn't want to sit down, he refused to do a wee so I said You're going to learn to pee like a big boy, and it made me laugh the way he stood on tiptoe holding his tiny little willy in his hands, it's funny how proud little boys are when they start peeing standing up.

When we went back into the bedroom Stan was already asleep with his clothes on in the double bed, and I suddenly thought He's only nine… so I ran my hand over his damp hair and I felt like kissing him, but I didn't, I didn't want to wake him, it's so unbelievable watching someone sinking into sleep, where does everybody go when they sleep, do they meet in their sleep, is there a kingdom of dreams, a real place, is it possible to land in someone else's dream, no, no, I mustn't start thinking like that, the psychiatrist at the health centre said, there are some ideas that take you straight to the bottom of the pit, he said, and I know he's right. Stan was just a little boy sleeping, that's what I should have thought, like the other mothers do before they switch the light off and go back down to finish the washing-up in the kitchen.

Are all three of us going to sleep in the same bed? asked Kevin, eyes wide with amazement, and I hadn't thought about that. Go to bed, I said, and before he asked for it I explained I'm going to give you a T-shirt, you can suck it like it was your noonoo, even if it doesn't smell the same, you're a big boy now, you do your wees standing up. But are we all sleeping in the same bed? he asked again, and I could tell he was really worried about it. No, of course not, I replied and I wondered once again what I was going to do. Go to bed, I said quietly, the bed's for Kevin and Stan. You're not going to leave us? he asked in a shrill panicky little voice like a girl's — like the first time I left him at school, I remember, Are you leaving? he asked, sort of horrified, and one of the mothers laughed when she heard him, her kid probably didn't love her anything like as much as mine loved me. I thought very fast and said I would sleep at the foot of the bed, I wouldn't even feel their feet because they always slept curled up, I knew that, I often watched them sleeping at night, they were almost bent double, like they were cold.

Kevin wanted his pyjamas, his "hotel pyjamas", the ones with Mickey Mouse on them, and it's funny how it reassured him putting them on, They smell like home, he said. Well, it's really worth the trouble taking them away! I thought, but the smell cheered me up, too, it smelt of my washing powder and of damp, the smell of my little boy, I put my head against his neck, necks are the softest bit on a child.

Kevin got into bed. The sheets aren't new, he said, all reproachful, and he was right! they weren't new at all, they were so worn they had holes, and some hadn't even been mended. They're clean, I said, but Kevin wasn't listening, he was wondering how he was going to cope with this strange noonoo, he sucked one corner of it, spat it out, sucked another, tasted it... Stop! I said, you'll make yourself thirsty, and where was I going to find a drink in that hotel? Given the state of the toilets, the plumbing must be a mess, and I didn't want my kids drinking rusty water.

When they were both asleep it was hard for me. The talking started all on its own in my head, I hate that, thinking is a nasty piece of work. Sometimes I'd rather be a dog, you can bet dogs never wonder what their place in life is or who they should follow, they just sniff the air and it's all recorded, in there for ever. And they stick to it. Humans don't have a sense of smell, that's what's dangerous. I'd like to be able to sniff around me and for everything to be clear, with just one meaning and no messing around. To stop the thinking I started humming a song, Brave sailor back from the war, Hushaby, my dad used to sing it when I was little, it used to make me cry, but it did me good now, singing an old song's like finding a long-lost friend. Brave sailor back from the war, Hushaby, Your boots all worn, your clothes all torn, Brave sailor where have you been, Hushaby! It's been the same sailor for thirty years, what I mean is the way I see him's still the same, he's still got his torn clothes and holes in his boots because it's the bit about "boots all worn" that really matters, it's terrible having sore feet, and shoes are the ruination of many a mother. I love saying that: many a mother! then heaving a sigh, overwhelmed, like the ones who wait at twenty-five past four, that's when you feel like you've got so much in common and might understand each other. For many a mother! mind you, you always have to sigh afterwards, never laugh, once with the social worker I got a fit of the giggles and when she took it badly I just couldn't stop, she looked like she was busy silently loathing me, I could tell I wasn't her favourite, I'm sure she'd rather lend her hanky than watch one of us have a good laugh.

Still, shoes *are* expensive. Tomorrow we'd be walking barefoot in the sand, we'd dip our feet in the water and laugh, so why couldn't I get to sleep, didn't even feel like singing any more. It's like that sometimes: everything brings me down, I don't know what to do with myself, what direction to point my dreams in, there must be paths I should follow, ones that aren't dangerous, well edged, that's right, with barriers everywhere, that's important.

I heard a noise in the room next door, voices, banging against the wall, how could I have thought the hotel was deserted? That's me all over, that is, when I'm on my own I think everyone's disappeared. It took me ages to recognize my neighbours! Years, I reckon. Now I've clocked them, they don't look unkind, but I still prefer going out when I can't hear anything in the corridor, when I'm sure I won't meet anyone. Of course there are some people I have to see. At the health centre, and school. I don't like it when Marie-Hélène asks to see me, Kevin may well be her pet, I know that, but she never gives praise, she's always asking questions, Why hasn't he got his plimsolls for gym? What time does he go to bed because he's falling asleep in lessons? Oh, that Marie-Hélène! Sometimes, when I want to frighten Kevin, I threaten him with her, I say I'll tell Marie-Hélène you didn't finish your mashed potato and you wet the bed again. Of course I won't, I won't tell Marie-Hélène, but when you're trying to bring up two kids on your own you need a bit of authority.

My boys were asleep. Curled up. Like kittens. Kevin's make-do noonoo was slipping out of his mouth, he always slept with his mouth open, because of his adenoids,

I always used to think that when I had the money I'd get him the operation but now... now...

I looked out the window, couldn't see a thing. I'm used to looking out at the buildings opposite and I like it, seeing people moving about behind their curtains and all the little lights coming on in the evening, it's pretty and we're all in the same boat, tucked away in our boxes, that's the way it should be, I like it. Here I couldn't see a thing, not even car headlights or a street lamp, nothing. What was it going to be like in broad daylight? What was there outside my window? The sea? No, I couldn't hear anything and anyway a hotel by the sea would have been too expensive, I'd have steered clear of that. So? What was facing me out there that I couldn't see? The bus station? A building site with cranes and lorries and all that racket, something being built or demolished? I hate that, houses torn in half, I can't stand seeing the colour of the wallpaper in houses half torn down, I can't think of anything sadder. Shouldn't have started trying to imagine it, everything was possible beyond that window, I had to be ready for anything, I should just forget it, forget it straight away before it gave me nightmares.

I got undressed, my clothes were soaked, rain, sweat, all smelly and stuck to my skin, but I didn't have the strength to go and wash at the far end of the corridor. I put on my nightdress and lay down at the foot of the bed, pulling the bedspread over me, it was cramped, we must have been quite a sight, the three of us huddled there! The three of us… That was nice to say, too. The children didn't move, I could hear them breathing, it was the first time I'd slept next to them and, hearing them breathing like that, I knew I was the one who'd given them that breath. Me. What a job life is… what a funny old job…

I thought about that and then went to sleep. I hadn't taken my medicine but no one sat on me that night. I was like everyone else that night. Tired by the journey and the emotion, and probably because I really couldn't think about what was coming next. I slept like I do during the day. Without dreams. Without pictures. Without feeling good or bad, perhaps without living, yes, I slept like the dead in that strange town, but still I knew that the next day my kids would have their first glimpse of the sea.

The next day was really bad luck, it was raining again. Apart from the dim morning light it was hard not getting day and night confused in that town. There wasn't much room for the light, no one had arranged for it, you could tell that right away. I don't know what the time was when I woke, but the kids were already up, they were by the window having a raindrop race: they each chose one at the top of a pane and the first to reach the bottom was the winner.

I wondered what they could see through the window, what the rain was hiding.

Mum! Kevin cried when he saw I was awake, and that's a wonderful thing! The way a littl'un says hello to you in the morning, as if you were the surprise of the day, the piece of good news he'd given up on. In the morning it was always like Kevin had missed me, I wonder where he goes at night to make him feel he's coming back from so far away. When it's a school day Stan won't let him into my room, I know that, but often on Sundays, when they've finished watching their cartoons, he doesn't hold back then, oh no, he jumps onto my bed and asks me to give him a farty kiss, that's a big kiss on his tummy which makes a lot of noise and it makes him laugh so much you wouldn't believe it, it's like he's laughing to hear himself laugh, that he's making the most of that laughter, having fun with it, and I know that a laugh like that runs away the minute you grow up.

I'm hungry! he said, and if there's one thing Kevin never forgets it's being hungry, sometimes I feel like a larder. We'll go to a café, I said, but neither of them looked convinced by that and I added We'll order and we'll be served! They looked at me suspiciously like I was telling a fib, so I got up and then I couldn't help smiling – never mind my gappy gums, I was too proud of myself, I rummaged through the blue sports bag, took out my tea tin and tipped it out onto the bed, regretting it didn't make more noise: I spilled out all my money! All of it! Everything I'd put by to have fun some day, all my little savings scrimped from the change at the baker and sometimes at the supermarket.

The kids didn't touch the money, they just looked at it, cautiously, like they were meeting someone new. Can we have an ice cream? Kevin asked to make sure, and I was convinced he was no longer missing school. Plonker! Stan said quietly, in a café you drink coffee! And, anyway, there's practically only twenty-centime coins left! Really? I said. Only twenty-centime coins? And I looked a bit closer. The boys sat down next to me on the bed, peering at my treasure like some strange creature. It's true there weren't many ten-franc coins, but hey! It was my scrimpings not an investment, a bit extra, okay! I didn't want them to see my disappointment, but at the same time I resented them for showing so little enthusiasm. Stan started counting the coins with such a serious expression you'd have thought he was picking up something I'd broken, sorting out some stupid accident, that's what they teach them at school: to be distrustful. Me, I've always had trouble managing my budget, I've got to admit there's not a lot to manage and also, as soon as I get my allowance, I celebrate, I mean I spend it. Not on me, no. On the kids. Always on the kids. Once one of the social workers asked me if I drank. Who? Me? Never touched a drop of alcohol, I mean, who the hell does she take me for, really! I rang the health centre like a shot and complained: Who did you send me? I asked, a social worker who thinks I drink! They apologized. That's how it works. Everyone's always waiting for you to put a foot wrong, for you to fall, it's like walking on soap, yes, our lives are full of soap, that's what I think.

There's fifty-two francs and thirty-five centimes, Stan announced. I've been had. Money isn't worth anything any more. Stan was right not to trust appearances, all those coins added together meant nothing. Kevin's convictions and happiness started wavering, Is that a lot? he asked, pulling a face… Yeah, I said nastily, specially with the thirty-five centimes, and it wasn't the littl'un I was annoyed with but the bloody money. Kevin gave a half-smile and said Great! and heaved a big sigh of relief. It's hard living up to a child's hopes. Right! I said, we're going to buy some biscuits and a bottle of water, and we're going to have a picnic down by the sea! It's raining, Stan said like it was my fault, and that was when I'd had enough. Nothing was working. Nothing was taking off. I asked them to play with the raindrops and went back to bed, but in the middle of it this time, not at the foot like an animal. The sheets were still all warm from the boys, I hugged the pillow to me and pulled the blankets over my head so I couldn't see anything, couldn't hear anything. Except I could still hear. Kevin was snivelling and stamping his feet, But I'm hungry! he kept saying and, however hard Stan tried to stop him, he kept at it.

I wanted to get back to the night before, that night without dreams or insomnia, the one that detached me from myself, I wanted to get back to that place with no threats that I'd fallen into, but I'd lost it for good. Did I have the same night as other people that time? Is this what they got every evening, a reward for getting through their day so well? I'm never rewarded and my sleep's like a knife hacking through the threads I cling to during the day. I'm abandoned. Dumped. And it started again. Instead of getting back to the night before, I went far and deep into my chilling black thoughts. I know them well. I didn't want to stay there, swimming in them and drowning. I could still hear the boys, I hung on to their voices, I had to get back up to where they were, to answer them. I sat up with a start, I didn't really know where I was, but I knew I had to stay. Here. In this room. I saw the kids, talking very quietly, looking out of the window, arguing without making a sound.

My Kevin! I cried, let's go and eat! And it became urgent, the only thing to do, and straight away: eat! eat! eat! That's what the rest of the world was doing, that's what you had to do to feel alive: eat! eat! eat! Let's get dressed and then we're off! I said. They didn't move, I got back into my clothes from the day before, they were cold and smelt horrible, I stayed under the covers to put them on… what if someone brought us breakfast up on a tray? It would be a miracle! Afterwards we'd go back to sleep, how wonderful! And why shouldn't the sea come to us too, yes, why shouldn't it come and settle at the foot of our bed, why shouldn't we be allowed that for once in our lives? If I could make a wish it would be this: for the sea to come to the foot of my bed. When I was little my father didn't only sing Brave Sailor Back from the War, he also sang a love song which said that in the middle of the bed the river runs deep and a hey and a ho, and that bed was a real princess's bed, a four-poster with hangings, not like in this brown hotel, oh no, you wouldn't get a river running through here, so the sea… forget it!

I like songs. They say things I can't seem to say. If I didn't have these rotten teeth I'd sing a lot more, a lot more often, I'd sing my boys to sleep in the evenings, tales of sailors and magical beds, but there you are, we can't be good at everything, we can't know how to do everything, all of it, that's what I tell the social worker till I'm blue in the face.

I got up. The lino was freezing, and sticky too. I wanted to see what was outside the window, but that wasn't possible because there was a wall on the other side of the window, a huge wall, and I wanted to know what was beyond the wall. Was it the back of a building, the back of a prison, the back of a changing room, and the far side there was a sun-filled meadow with kids playing ball games, hmm? What was it? Another hotel for this town nobody lives in, a place everyone comes and sniffs around for a few days before leaving again on the bus? Ha! No point thinking about it, it was just a bloody great sun-block, a life-block, a fucking concrete wall, I didn't want to look at it any more, or try to find out its secrets.

You look like a couple of old rags, I told the boys, I bet you haven't washed. I showed Stan how I can pee standing up, said Kevin. Oh, yes, I said, well, the bathroom's right next door, why didn't you nip in there, hmm? Stan says there's creepy-crawlies, muttered Kevin, wrinkling his nose. Creepy-crawlies don't eat great big things like you, Stan, didn't you tell him that? And now you look like a couple of pigs. Stan stared at the end of his trainers and said he didn't want me to wake up all alone. Well I never! How does he know, my Stan, how does he know I often feel lost when I wake up? He must spy on me, unbelievable but yes, like when I sit for hours in the kitchen and he waits behind the door. Does my little boy watch me sleeping? And who's going to watch me sleeping tomorrow?

You've got to wash your faces at least, I ordered, and they seemed to like that. I've noticed how kids love doing what they're told, what everyone else is doing. Sometimes Stan even lays it on a bit, saying things like We have to brush our teeth after every meal. Oh yeah? And where did you see that? On the telly? No, my teacher said it. God, you wouldn't believe the power they have, those teachers, they could make them eat anything, they could tell them to walk on their hands and for sure there'd be no more spending a fortune on shoes!

We slipped quietly along the corridor but the bathroom was occupied. Right, this hotel wasn't deserted at all, there were even people where we wanted to be, soon we'd be queuing to have a pee. What time was it? Were people getting ready to go to work? Were they smartening up to go to work? Why? Funny, it annoyed me not knowing who was shaving in there, or who was slapping it all over her face, make-up everywhere she could possibly put it, eyes cheeks mouth, the whole lot, and us stuck in the corridor waiting our turn!

I'm hungry, Kevin said again like they were the only words he knew, so I decided that was enough, my kids didn't look like rags or pigs, I'd said that to be like all the other mothers, the ones who look for creepy-crawlies and want everything to be perfect, deep down I thought my boys were gorgeous and what was a bit of cold water going to do for us?

I hadn't come here to hang around while strangers washed their faces!

We went back to our room and they got dressed, Kevin had always worn Stan's old clothes, and Stan clothes that were too big so that they lasted, and I'd never noticed that neither of them had things the right size. True, I'm not there when they get ready in the mornings, but now I could see that they didn't look like the others, two little lads, one too big and the other too small. Did they know that?

We put on our jackets, I gathered up the coins we'd abandoned on the bed and stuffed them into our pockets. I was really disappointed, mind, I thought I had much more, I'd even pictured myself saying Keep the change! to waiters and shopkeepers. I'd seen that done once, and then the person who's meant to keep the money looks at you like they wanted to kiss your feet, they were definitely going to keep it, that change! There I was thinking I had a treasure... money should be worth what we want it to be.

I've got lots of money! said Kevin, weighing up his pocket, but Stan shrugged his shoulders. Shame, I was prepared to believe it. Once again we left the room one behind the other, slipping through the half-open door, I felt like I'd been doing that all my life – slipping through things, I mean.

The stairs were easier going this way, but just as dark. Kevin had fun going down with both feet together, I could tell he was happy. Stan looked at the numbers on the doors, the arrows, the emergency exits, Stan always tries to read any writing, everywhere, ever since Year 1 he's wanted to make everything out, I don't know what he's looking for. I was wondering what we would find downstairs, what daylight would do to this town, would we see some pavements at last and some street names?

Each wrapped up in our thoughts, separated by them, we reached the ground floor without even realizing it and not out of breath, like relaxed travellers, tourists ready to explore the town. Shame there was no one in the foyer, I'm sure I looked a picture with my two boys.

The town was like the hotel: not deserted at all. Unbelievable how many people there were milling around in the rain, I was stunned. I had no idea what time it was and I didn't know what was driving these people in every direction. Life, it's an anthill! People hurry along, they brush past each other, knock into each other, every now and then they swear at someone or kiss hello, How are you? Fine! And then they watch all the others walking by.

No one was looking at us three, standing stock-still in the rain, hard to know which way to go to find a café. I decided to do what I did the night before: act like I knew what I was doing. What matters is looking like you know.

The roads were still just as muddy, the ground was sodden but no one paid attention. These people weren't out for a stroll, oh no, they were trotting along busily, not looking up but not getting lost either. They all looked like they had somewhere to go, they seemed to know the way by heart. I set off at random, in my I-know-what-I'm-doing mode, the kids trusted me and that brought me luck because guess what we came to? You'd have thought it was expecting us! The sea, yes, the sea! Bang in the middle of town, now that's something. You're looking for a café and you find the ocean, that doesn't happen every day, it was quite a surprise.

I stopped on the sea wall, my two kids holding my hands, I wondered how to do it, how to say hello to the sea. It was making a hellish noise, really angry, and the children cowered. I stayed there, not moving a muscle, watching it… I'd been waiting for it such a long time! Will it come right up to us? Kevin asked. Of course! Stan teased, it's going to come right up and shake your mit! Really? said the littl'un… My God! Children really are prepared to believe anything, I could have admitted to him that I dreamt of seeing the sea at the foot of my bed.

I've got to say Kevin was frightened out of his tiny mind, not at all in the mood for looking for shells or running through the lapping waves – lapping waves were thin on the ground, these were huge great waves stretching out furiously, not something you wanted to get close to. It wasn't very inviting and the rain didn't help. It really did look like it was coming towards us, at least it was trying to, gathering itself up, building the waves high to reach us and then falling back down… it was up to us to get closer. We'd better move, I told the kids, we'll dissolve in all this water, and down we went onto the beach, the littl'un still wary, I could tell from the way he squeezed my hand, he'd have been happier backing away, that's for sure, and landing safe and warm in the classroom with Marie-Hélène, him being her favourite.

The sea had lost all its colour, it wasn't blue at all, it looked like a torrent of mud, it was the same colour as the sky, what I mean is even the beach was like the hotel: same feeling of being in a cardboard box. It's completely blue, really, I told Kevin, but it was making such a row he didn't hear me – maybe I didn't actually say it, maybe I was talking to myself, It's breathing very loud! Kevin shouted, tugging at my arm. Don't be scared, I said, it's just saying how glad it is to see you, it's really missed you! Does it know me? The whole world knows you, Kevin, that's what I wanted to say, the whole world's waiting for you, but that was wrong, I know there's no one waiting for us. But aren't we allowed to lie every now and then, to turn ourselves into fairies, children expect it and it gives them a chance to dream, what's wrong with that?

Does it know me? Kevin shouted again, I nodded but I think he'd already stopped looking at me, he'd taken a sharp step back because a wave had come and licked at his shoes.

Stan was a little way away now, running all over the beach like something was chasing him. He's not right, that lad, I thought, it was like he was trying to get away from something, the rain, the cold, some imaginary creature, it was strange, he'd run with his head down, then stop suddenly as if there was a wall, then set off again just as quickly, turn to the right, turn to the left... what was he thinking right then, what sort of world was he in, I couldn't say. I would have liked him to stop but I didn't have the strength to run after him, my head was spinning horribly, I sat down on a rock, Kevin started playing with the wet sand at my feet, he'd lost interest in the sea. I couldn't help looking at it, though, wanted to be like it, self-contained, not giving a stuff about anything and taking up as much space as I liked. It's conceited alright, it isn't friendly, it's conceited, we come all this way to see it and if it could it would grind us into the ground, freeze the air in our lungs and fill our mouths with water if we got too close, and the waves were like huge mouths snapping at the empty air, waiting for us, just us.

Stan! I cried, Stan! Come back now! But he carried on running into his walls, so I went over to him, tripping on stones but not taking my eyes off him, while the waves smacked at the empty air behind him. Stan! I cried again, but even when I reached him he acted deaf, carrying on with his turns and half-turns, it drove me mad, I grabbed him by the hood of his jacket and then something terrible happened, Stanley raised his hand and thumped my arm, and I let go of his hood. He'd never ever done anything like that to me, There's the future, I thought, misery goes on for ever. I didn't recognize my little boy, we looked at each other in silence, he was red in the face, exhausted, wide-eyed, breathing heavily, like he was crying without any tears. Go home now! I shouted. And he looked me right in the eye. Go home, go home, obviously that was stupid, there was nowhere to go home to, I knew that and I was the one who ended up looking away. We stayed there like that without a word, catching our breath, trying to recognize each other while behind us the sea battered the sand. We weren't out for a stroll on this beach, we were hunting each other down, that was all.

I went back over to Kevin, Stan followed. We both felt ashamed. We didn't speak. Kevin was making sand-castles, I sat back down on the rock, Stan just stood there with his hands in his pockets, staring at the waves, exhausted, he'd been fighting with the sea too.

It's an enchanted castle, Stan! said Kevin, tugging the bottom of his brother's trousers, it's an enchanted castle! The older boy didn't look at the littl'un, still star-ing at the ocean, like they had unfinished business. Find him a seashell, Stan, I told him, just to say something, to show him I was there, even if I was worried he would walk away. He heard me. He didn't answer, but as he walked off along the sand he looked so alone, I felt like calling him back, how could he cope so well without me?

It's an enchanted castle, Kevin told me, slightly an-noyed. Yeah, it's good, it's good to make castles by the seaside, I thought, that's what's supposed to happen, we're by the seaside and we make sandcastles, that's what's always supposed to happen: the way it is... but why's Stan going so far away? Should I have smacked him when he thumped my arm? Should I have run after him and punished him? Maybe we should have had a fight, there, on the wet sand, rolling on the ground and biting each other, scratching and roaring, drowning out the waves, more like monsters than the ocean itself, forgetting about being a mother and son, just thumping each other, and then feeling better afterwards.

Stan was walking along the beach but he wasn't looking for shells, that's for sure. He was looking ahead, at that little rain-swept beach, with its stones and bits of black seaweed, its abandoned bottles and plastic bags snagged on the rocks, he was walking slowly, like someone thinking about something and lugging their tiredness with them. I'd like to have been inside his head, right in the depths of him, so that no one else could take that space, my space, me, the first… the first what, I don't know, but the first, yes, that was it… I'm in him, on the inside, even if he doesn't know it.

I'm cold, Kevin said, I'm cold and I'm hungry, can we go? Good idea, actually, let's go, got to go, have to go and have something to drink, got to. Come back, Stan! I cried – nothing in the world would have made me go over to him. Come back! I yelled, it felt good, Come back! Come back! I was an order, I was a shout, but the waves swallowed my words, you'd have thought the sea was a machine, it made more din than a factory.

Stan didn't hear me. I no longer existed. I had no voice left, no more words, nothing could reach him. I stopped shouting. Stan's outsize clothes were moving all on their own in the wind, he reminded me of a boat. I didn't know how to bring boats back in.

Kevin had had enough. He shouted now, and then ran over to his brother, he took his hand and they walked towards me, they were soaked, the pair of them. There are my boys, I thought, two ice cubes melting away, you'd have thought I made them out of water, and they've just come out of the sea.

I was no longer angry with Stan, and when he reached me I took his hand, too. Walking through that town without pavements it was more reassuring holding hands, the three of us.

It *was* a nice feeling stepping into that café. We weren't exactly cheerful, not at our best, but it felt good. The heating was on – happiness hangs on virtually nothing, a bit of heating after the rain and life opens up a little.

We took off our jackets and sat down on a bench seat, and then I thought I shouldn't have gone all that way to see the sea, but just gone to a café, I should have left the sea to the kids, one last dream. In the summer it's all blue, I said, they looked at me but didn't understand. Kevin was worried, I don't like coffee, what can I have? Whatever you like, I replied. A coke? he leapt up from the seat as he said it, he was happy and it was lovely seeing him like that, but still, I wasn't going to spend all my money on coke, he'd still be complaining he was hungry afterwards. Have a hot chocolate, I said, it stays by you longer, and he shot me a sulky look from beneath his eyebrows.

Stan was listening to the men leaning up at the bar. They were having quite a laugh, with their cigarettes in their mouths and their beers in their hands, they were talking dirty and I didn't want Stan to hear it, I was embarrassed like I had something to do with their vulgar words – a bit like when the two of us watch TV together, yes, like that evening when I felt so ashamed, I still remember it, because a man who'd just won crazy amounts of money in some game started gasping and whooping and ended up rolling around on the ground shouting. I didn't like seeing that with my son, I can't explain why.

No, I didn't want Stan listening to the men at the bar, they were talking about a woman, and I bet she wasn't one of their wives, they were laughing and scratching their bellies, one of them started burping and one of the others laughed so much he had a coughing fit. It wasn't so nice after all in that café, and I couldn't wait to get out. I can't seem to stay in the same place for long, there's always something that upsets me or makes me sick. Usually people make me sick. I wish they could be more like kids: with more questions than answers, but it's often the other way round, where did they learn to be so sure of everything?

The owner came over, I asked him how much it would cost to have one coke, two hot chocolates and a coffee, Forty-two francs, he said after thinking for a moment with his eyes turned to the ceiling. That's fine, I said, that's what we'll do, will the straw be for free if we have a straw with the coke? He slipped back to the bar without answering, his feet thumping heavily on the floor, it was like he'd just got out of bed and was having trouble walking.

Is the coke for me? Kevin asked, and he rubbed his hands together. He's already imitating grown-ups, I thought, and I wondered how long a child could go on being his mother's son, exactly when he became unrecognizable, I mean: just like the others. Exactly when? The men at the bar with their bellies shaking as they coughed, with their dirty ideas about women's arses, were those men still somebody's son? You have to drink the hot chocolate first, I said to make myself think about something else. But after I can have the coke! he said and his little feet drummed gleefully against the seat. You're spoilt, aren't you? Really spoilt! I wanted to talk to him, had to talk to stop myself thinking about the men at the bar. Normally it's Stan I talk to, but since he'd thumped my arm it was difficult. And, anyway, he hadn't found a seashell. We wouldn't be going back to the beach, I knew that, Kevin would never take a present back for Marie-Hélène... I heard the men laughing, I think they'd stopped making fun of the woman and moved on to a goalie. Maybe it's the same thing. We're on our own. We wait there and take the blows without complaining. The others watch.

In the summer it's all blue, I said again, you can sit on the sand eating ice cream and it melts on your fingers in the heat. Have you done that? Kevin asked me, brimming with pride... I hesitated... Yes, I said eventually, yes I've done it, and more than once, I've died of the heat by the sea before now, I've seen it when it's all blue, with the sky overhead like a huge mirror... more than once... I would have liked Stan to believe it, too, to ask me questions, but I didn't know what the little smile he gave me meant, did he think my story was nice, did he think I was managing it well and that I was full of wonderful memories that would make them drool with envy?

The owner came back, dragging his feet on the ground even more. He put the drinks on the table with a sigh, there was a straw in the glass of coke – maybe he liked children but didn't dare show it because of the men at the bar watching him, waiting for the chance to burst out laughing, I could feel it – like I would do them that favour, what the hell did they think? Bloody hell! I'd forgotten how much men depend on us to have a good laugh together, I'd forgotten how it weighs you down having them look you over. Very happy to be on my own with my kids. No more You're letting yourself go! Make an effort! No more living like I was on display in a shop window, apparently... yes, apparently in some northern country the tarts sit in shop windows. Sometimes I wonder what difference that makes. Except that they're paid, of course. When it's over, when the men have done what they needed to do, it feels like nothing's happened, men never remember it, maybe that's why it has to keep happening again. A bit of money thrown in at the end does leave a trace, a bit of proof – we're owed that, at least: a bit of recognition.

Kevin drank his hot chocolate through the straw, Stan called him a plonker, I was pleased to see him back in the land of the living, Leave him alone, I said, if it makes him happy. Sometimes I like seeing Kevin fooling about, it reassures me. There are times when I fool about as well to make them laugh. I do impersonations for them. They get them every time because it's always the same people: the woman who lives along the corridor who takes tiny steps when she walks, like a Chink, with that horrified look on her face, like she's trying to avoid some dustbins; the cashier at the supermarket with her octopus hands, her snooty expression and her huge tits; the pediatrician at the health centre, always waving a needle, we call him Doctor Dart and once Kevin actually said Bye, Doctor Dart! Stan and I were embarrassed but the quack proved he never listens to a word you say because he put his hand on the kid's head and muttered Well done, my boy, well done, as he opened the door for us to leave. Anyway, all that just to say that sometimes the three of us have fun. We have good times. It's only very brief, I never know where it comes from, but I know it's good, the world around us takes up a bit less space, our shoulders feel lighter. It's when we're not talking to each other that we understand each other best, and when we fool around, too. But the kids are better behaved than me. I bet if I'd impersonated Doctor Dart in the café they'd have been ashamed of me. Like when I pull faces behind people's backs if I don't like them. They hate it. In fact, the kids are frightened of other people.

I can't fault them for that. You're never what they want you to be. You irritate them, disgust them. The whole world's disappointed by its neighbours. Sometimes, no one knows why, someone exactly matches what everyone expected. And everybody loves them, they cheer them and put them on the telly. It's very rare. The rest of the human race is all mistrust and hate, what I mean is love's nothing like as common as hate.

After the chocolate Kevin drank the coke and of course he wanted a wee. I asked Stan to go with him, he refused. What? I said, you're nine years old and you can't take your brother for a piss? At the time I didn't think he might be frightened of passing the men at the bar, in fact I was panicking that he might still resent me for what happened on the beach and I snapped at him, You're off your rocker! I regretted it. It hurt him. He opened his mouth like he was going to speak, looked up at me with his little eyes, then turned his head sharply towards the window, like he wanted to hide. I'm desperate! said Kevin, and he couldn't work out which of us he should be talking to.

I got up, took him by the hand and stormed to the back of the café, when we passed them the men at the bar turned round and suddenly stopped talking, and one of them came out with Isn't there school today? as if he knew that would upset the littl'un the most. Neither of us said anything. I couldn't wait to get back to the hotel. For no one to be watching us. For no one to talk to us.

The toilet was tiny and dark, with crates of empty bottles stacked right outside, there was sawdust on the floor and cigarette butts, it smelt of red wine and damp. Lucky that Kevin had learnt to pee standing up. There's school today, what are we going to tell Marie-Hélène? he asked me... and that was when I started thinking about it, too, in that stink of booze and half-stubbed cigarettes... I wondered what they would tell her, what they would tell Marie-Hélène... Will you write a note? the littl'un asked as he zipped up his flies. That's right, I said, I'll write a note. It reassured him. There are magic sentences like that. I'll write a note.

When we got back to our table Stan had started counting the money, he'd taken the coins from our jacket pockets and was making little piles. Everyone was watching him, and as I passed the bar the owner turned towards me, shot me a nasty look and nodded his head as if to say What's that boy up to? What's going on? We've... we've got a lot of change, I said, and Shit! my voice had run off again, it was like not all of me was there, like I'd left a bit at home. All the men at the bar hitched their balls up and turned to look at me, this wasn't looking good, they were far too interested in us, didn't they have anything better to do?

The owner came out from behind his counter and slouched on over to Stan. The kid was very calm, very busy with his coins, so lost in his own world he couldn't even see us. But the owner was right up close to him now, with a nasty, nosy look in his eye. Come and have a look at this! he said to the others, and that was exactly what they'd been waiting for, this bunch of alcoholics, they rushed over to the table as if a baby had just been born there. That's it, I thought, it's too late. I wanted to spare them all this, but it was going too fast for me, my kids had seen the fury of the sea and now they were going to see how hostile the world is, this town was the beginning of hell.

The men stood round Stan, like a pack of dogs, I could tell they were ready to pounce as soon as he gave the word. He knew it. He took his time. He made it last. Stan, my Stan with his nice manners was still just as calm. He carried on with his little piles: one-franc coins, fifty-centime coins, twenties, tens… I admired him, I really did. With one swipe of his hand the owner toppled the lot. The others laughed and one of them, still the same one, he started coughing, his belly heaved up and down, and he farted. Stan looked up at the owner, no longer so sure of himself, stunned, yes that was it, he still didn't realize what was going on. Kevin gave a tiny, sad little groan, he doesn't like it when people have a go at his brother, I made a desperate effort to speak and I said, We've only got change. I would have liked my voice to be very loud, way more posh than that café but it was pathetic, almost begging. But coins are still money, aren't they? They could make the forty-two francs, no problem, they could even have managed a tip, we were good customers, four drinks in one round, that's not to be sniffed at!

The owner looked disgusted, he looked at the scattered money like he'd never seen anything so dirty, but what could he do to us? He wanted us to pay and we were paying, only those men were watching him, and he felt it was all up to him. So he hoiked up his belt with both hands and then with this outraged expression he said, Come on, come on clear all this away! and waved his hand around over the table. The men clicked their tongues, it was like a group of good honest people facing a pack of hooligans, and the hooligans were us.

The owner went back to his bar, stooped and heavy-footed, the game was over. The men were sorely disappointed, you could tell, looking pretty stupid now it was all over, now there was nothing else they could wring out of us and, nodding their heads like a bunch of disgruntled little old women, they followed the owner back to the bar, going home to their kennels. One of them asked Isn't there school today? again and the others started sniggering, why did they hate us so much, I didn't get it.

Stan gathered up the coins and we put our jackets on, they were soaking and when I put mine on my whole body started shivering, I tensed myself to fight off the cold and wet, I hurt all over. Kevin took his brother's hand again, like on the beach, like he was the one who had to bring him safely back each time, his big brother had taught him that: taking care of someone.

We left without saying goodbye, but the men had lost interest in us anyway, the owner had bellowed It's my round! and they were all holding their glasses up to a bottle of white wine, a gift from the gods, as far as they were concerned.

It was still raining outside, the same icy monotonous rain, this town had no imagination, it could only do rain. Stan said he knew the way back to the hotel, I think he was lying because we went past the post office three times, but I didn't say anything because I was too tired, more wrung out than after a sleepless night and, by going round in circles, we eventually found our hotel, our brown hotel.

It felt welcoming to me, it did, a bolthole, a burrow in this strange place, but on the way up the stairs Kevin said he wanted the seashell to give to Marie-Hélène, as if we could dig one up now from the lino, as if we could go back to that angry beach. He said he wanted it, he cried for it like he would have cried for Marie-Hélène, and Stan let go of his hand sharply. The littl'un was surprised and he gave him a kick on the shin before running off crying. Be quiet! Just shut up! I said, do you want to draw attention to us? Why was I so frightened? Apart from the person in the bathroom, you couldn't tell there was anyone in the hotel and, anyway, I didn't give a stuff about invisible neighbours, what frightened me wasn't someone hearing my two kids laying into each other, no, what frightened me was this violence they'd kept in check and couldn't hold back any more. They settled it by pulling faces at each other, I could tell they really wanted to fight, to yell at each other, incredible how you can go from love to hate, there's never any warning, there's like an irritation, a fury that builds up and you don't really know who or what it's aimed at, sometimes I wish I could scream, to find who it is I've got it in for, but there are no limits and everything's against me.

I was shattered, I hurt all over and I wanted to go to bed, I'd seen too much already. I *was* shattered but I was actually happy we had to climb all that way, right to the sixth floor, we were getting away from the mud, the sea, the cafés, the roads without pavements. I could have climbed even higher and even faster.

When we reached our room my hand shook with impatience as I opened the door, that bed was a miracle on earth, I took off my jacket and my muddy shoes and threw myself onto it. I got under the sheets and told the kids, I don't want to hear another word, and I closed my eyes, I wanted to get right inside myself, where nothing more could reach me. The kids are used to it. I often sleep all day on a Sunday. They sort themselves out. They poke about in the fridge, watch TV, and when it's fine they go out to play. But in that room there was nothing to do, nowhere to put yourself, so they played with the coins. I could hear them and then, pretty soon, it worked, at last, at last, I went.

I left everything, left that town and myself along with it: my body was weightless, painless, I sank into something soft and I shed my fear and anger, and my shame too. I went to a world where there's a place kept for me. Not asleep and not awake, I'm a feather. Not asleep and not awake, but I come undone, I sprawl out like a cotton reel unwinding. Why did I topple over the edge then? Why did I start to dream?

I dreamt of the sea, I remember, of Stan running towards the sea, into the sea, but not drowning, and me with no words left to call him back... Where was Kevin? I don't know, I could feel him but not see him, it was like the sea was only there for Stan and the two of them understood each other so well that it couldn't hurt him. When we understand them, things are good to us, they're on our side, as soon as there's any confusion, I've noticed, as soon as we don't understand them, things hurt us. I kept looking out for Stan, trying to spot him way out to sea, wanting him so badly but unable to speak, and sleep was no longer a refuge, just a place. A place where anything can happen, anything can pounce on you, and you go down, you go down somewhere deep, no one to catch you, you just keep falling. I went there. Crushed. Punished. Worn down.

When I woke up it was almost dark in the room, the sky was full of black clouds, the weather had taken a

turn for the worse. I had four boys: the ones in my sleep
and the ones in the room, beside me. The four of them
didn't know each other, I was the only one who got them
confused, who knew about getting from one world to
the other, and the pain that always lurked in between.

The boys had stopped playing and were lying on the
bed: Kevin sucking his make-do noonoo and winding
a lock of hair round his finger, and Stan watching me,
I think. He smiled at me, he never resents me for sleeping, he knows I'm better after, when I've had a chance
to "recharge the batteries", as I call it. I didn't tell him a
nightmare had just cut me right to the quick, I'd rather
believe I was fine, too, I'd had a good nap, we agreed
on that. Maybe it's the tiredness that's made me lose
touch with everyone else. I couldn't spend a full day on
my feet, doing this and that, being friendly, polite and
happy, no, I wouldn't make it through a whole day with
my eyes open. Shame sleep has two sides to it: it's a way
of forgetting but also a threat. No way of knowing in
advance which side you're going to fall on. I believe in
it every time, I always hope it's not going to be such a
struggle as being awake, I'm often wrong.

The insomnia got worse when Stan was born. I
started listening out for him: crying, breathing, coughing. I thought I had to stand guard, that if I went to
sleep he'd play a nasty trick on me, I know it happens,
children dying, all alone, in their cots. It was the same
with Kevin, of course, and now that they're both bigger
I still keep watch, sometimes I tell myself the whole city

needs guarding, that there has to be a light on somewhere. Apparently there are these priests, no, not priests,
monks. Apparently there are these monks who pray for
the sorrows of the world, day and night, never stopping,
taking it in shifts so there's never a break. Me, I don't
know how to pray. I'd rather not believe in God, it's too
frightening and, anyway, how can I understand God
when I don't understand his representative, the Pope,
that rich, crumbly old man? God must be like a bunch
of popes put together, thousands of popes in one single
person, terrifyingly powerful... yes, but knowing there
are these monks thinking of me night and day, that's
reassuring.

Kevin's hungry, Stan said. I'll go down and buy some
biscuits, put the coins back in the tea tin, I told him. Are
you going to pay with those little coins? He was worried,
you'd have thought I was going to rob a bank. I'm not
going to hang on to my savings, Stan, I put them aside
for this trip, I've got to spend them. He put the money
back in the tin, judging by the noise it made you'd have
thought there was a lot of it, but it was dead money,
money no one trusted, I'd grasped that.

Kevin was sucking on his noonoo more and more
quickly, his eyes closing, opening, closing again, he was
falling asleep, he felt safe. Keep an eye on your brother,
Stan, I said... It was so obvious Stan would keep an
eye on the littl'un, I don't know why I needed to say it,
some sentences are just like that. Be careful when you
cross the road, Don't talk to strangers, Keep an eye on

your brother, such simple sentences, they belong to everyone and we say them all the time so they never go out of circulation. Our parents used to say them. And our parents' parents. They're sacred, compulsory, make you feel alive.

I put my sodden jacket and muddy shoes back on, and left the two of them on their own.

As I went down the stairs I realized I was leaving them in another world, a bubble about to burst. The further down I went, the closer I got to hell. The hell of other people. Of course, I have to go there every now and then, there are things I need to get. It must be like this in war: breaking cover, risking your life to survive. Kevin was hungry. And Stan, too, I was sure he was. Not me. I was poisoned, full of bile and sour saliva, the sea salt had got into my mouth.

I went down those stairs, and the mist gathered a little closer round me with each floor, I missed steps, thinking they were further down than they were, falling slightly each time, like air pockets in the middle of a dream. With all that missing steps and seeing them too close or too far, my head started spinning, I clung to the banister, I could feel myself lurching to one side, someone must be pushing me from behind, I was sure they were. I stopped on one floor, I don't remember which, they were all the same – brown, lit only by the neon of the fire exit signs, maybe that's what was making me ill, all those endless floors, it drove me mad. My head was throbbing like the blood couldn't wait to get out, I was out of breath. I'm used to that. It's not the tiredness, it's the panic. I've told them about it at the health centre. I'm not the only one, it does happen to people. You've got to reason with yourself. That's what they say. In fact, all their sentences start like that: You've got to. It sounded to me like: You forgot to, you forgot to, you forgot to. Right! I couldn't reason with myself, so the only way to deal with it was to piss off out of there as fast as possible and I hurtled down the stairs, with my fears chasing after me. Of course I tripped and twisted my wrist clinging on to the banister, I was like a ball thrown down from one of the upper floors, I bounced and I bumped but all the same... I reached the bottom.

A feeling of having come a long, long way, my kids were far away from me now, a whole journey lay between us. There was a leatherette armchair in the foyer, and I slumped down into it. I should have felt relieved, proud of myself, proud of winning that round, but I felt worse by the minute. It must have shown. A man came over, probably the hotel manager, I didn't see him coming, he startled me. I couldn't actually make him out very well, I was dazzled, like when the sun's too bright, but the sun had abandoned that town long ago.

My heart felt all heavy and full, sort of thick, every beat hurt, it was full of blood, keeping hold of it and not letting it out any more, my hands and mouth started tingling, the manager seemed to be talking to me, I could hear but it sounded so far away, there were tons of cotton wool between us, it absorbed everything, every word and even the air, I was short of air, I hadn't brought my pills.

I had to hang on to something, an idea, an image, something to get me out of this, I was a wonky machine, jumping in every direction, little twitches, nerves waking up with a jolt around my eyes, my hands, my lips, they moved on their own, twisting for no reason, turning inwards and biting themselves all on their own, the man shook my shoulder and then it came. In fits and starts. A bit at a time. But it came. I honestly believe that's what saved me. Tears, moaning, more tears, little yelps, I couldn't do anything to stop all that. The manager backed away quickly and left, maybe he was frightened I'd splatter him. Well, fine. I'd rather be left in peace, unhappiness is never a pretty sight.

I let my rickety machine run its course and, gradually, everything went back in to place. I was spent, I'd been beaten and battered every which way. I stayed in that chair for a while, to recover: my heart, my nerves, my muscles, it all had to start up again gently, without bumping into anything, without going mad, calmly, and back to normal. A huge sigh came out of my chest, one final misfire, and I knew I could set off again. I stood up, pushing off against the chair, my head was still spinning a bit but everything else seemed to be working. The manager came back. A problem? he asked. I knew exactly what I must have looked like, I was used to it: red face, thick nose, dark rings under my eyes and white lips. On top of that, I smelt bad, rain and sweat didn't make a good combination. A problem? he repeated, slightly irritated. Everything's fine, I said, stressing both words to be sure they didn't get away from me, and I added, I'm off to do my shopping, trying to sound casual. Why did he have to look at me like that? Hadn't he ever seen anyone cry? Where do people cry? I often wonder about that, funny you never see people blubbing in the street. They make phone calls much more than they cry, maybe we'd hate each other less if we cried a bit more.

I walked towards the door, as upright as I could manage, the bloke stepped aside, frightened I'd fall on him, poor git! I knew exactly what I was doing. I wouldn't have asked him the way to the nearest shop for anything in the world, I do have my pride. Just as I was about to go out he called, There's a funfair on, you should take your boys! Now, that was a good idea! We'd make up for the grey sea and the scrap in the café, we'd have our bright lights! A funfair? Uh-huh, he said, on the outskirts of town, just before the main road. I was too exhausted to carry on the conversation so I gave him a little wave and went out.

Hard to say whether it was nightfall already or whether it had never actually been day, the light itself seemed so hesitant. It wasn't raining so hard but the sky was darker, it was a fine rain with tiny icy raindrops, poor man's snow, something you couldn't put a name to. It did me good, though. I tipped my head back and looked directly at the sky, it was all fresh, waiting for me.

In fact, the town was very small, everything was either at the end of the road or behind the post office, it was a shrunken town, maybe the sea nibbled into it a bit more each day, edging a bit further into the streets. I walked very slowly through the mud, it was harder on your own than with a kid on each hand. It's just as well they're not here, I thought, they didn't see me cry, the psychiatrist often says Try to avoid breaking down in front of the children. Right. There are some things you have to do in secret. You forgot to, forgot to, forgot to.

I didn't have any trouble finding a shop. There were wizened vegetables and black bananas displayed by the door, they didn't seem to be attracting any customers, and the shopkeeper was outside the door watching all those people walking past and not stopping at his shop. Mind you, he didn't look very pleased to see me, he barely budged to let me pass, and then he followed me inside looking at the mud I was leaving on the floor. Terrible weather! he said. I didn't answer. They say it's not getting better. I couldn't give a stuff, he'd never guess how little I cared. I chose some chocolate biscuits and a bottle of water – incredible how much they charge for their water, you'd never know it just falls out the sky.

At the till I pulled the tea tin from my pocket, it wasn't easy and the shopkeeper watched me with a frown, which was a good start... Okay! Stay calm, darlin', I thought, this bloke doesn't exist, he's just a shadow, he can't do anything to you. I took out my ridiculous coins and said, This is all they had at the bank, can you imagine? He opened his eyes so wide! Like he'd never seen money before in his life, This had to happen to me, he muttered, and I knew straight away he couldn't wait for someone else to come into the shop to make fun of me. Tough luck, the place was deserted, and he started counting the money, all disdainful like he didn't really want it, my arse! I was his only customer that month, he could at least have thanked me. I told myself all that to keep going, but I was dying to bugger off out of there. Let him take the money and let me never see him again. People can come into your life like that, from one moment to the next, even if you don't want them to. You should be able to screen them. Why was I alone with this tight-fisted shopkeeper when my kids were waiting for me up there? He put the money in the till, I stuffed everything into a plastic bag and left without saying goodbye.

Still no light outside, same rain, same people, I think it was the ones I'd seen earlier still going round in circles, was it really that dismal where they lived that they had to dawdle like this before going home? What were they after in town that they couldn't find in their own homes? Me, I couldn't wait to get inside, had enough of exposing my face to the air.

When I got back to the hotel the manager was no longer there, the phone was ringing all on its own and there was a smell of sausages, he must have been making a little snack, I wondered what time it could realistically be, was this dinner or tea?

Those stairs were pure torture, I looked at the tips of my toes to stop feeling dizzy, the bottle of water weighed a ton and, when I reached the third floor and realized I was only halfway up, I was so disheartened I sat down and started singing a song to myself, just to have something else to think about. Brave sailor back from the war, Hushaby, your shoes all worn, your clothes all torn, Brave sailor where have you been, Hushaby. I thought about how tired that sailor was, how tired the whole world was, we were all exhausted, weren't we? Who felt like getting up in the morning? If people weren't paid any more, wouldn't half the world stay in bed? Not necessarily... sailors love the sea, even when it's grey, even when it's nasty, and soldiers love war... even in the snow, even in the mud... I'm the only one who's so exhausted, didn't I use to long to be knocked down by a car and break my leg so I'd finally have a good enough reason to be left in peace? When am I going to be left in peace? I'm just missing a few chemicals, yes, that's what I tell myself when I swallow my pills, I've got fewer chemicals than other people... maybe it's that simple, maybe that's all it is: a few more chemicals... a few less... Brave sailor back from the war, Hushaby... it's the Hushaby that makes it seem tired, that song, when a man's really hushed he's bound to stop. To stop laughing and putting on airs, I mean he can just forget it. There's nothing better than a man who can forget it, and there's nothing so bloody rare, either. You find it mostly in songs, and films, in everything you can't touch. Dear lady, I'm back from the war… Dear lady, I'm back from the war… I stood up and climbed the remaining floors counting the steps, there were thirty-six of them, thirty-six little numbers to count between my kids and me.

Stan had locked the door, I knocked, he opened it very gently, he didn't look welcoming but when he saw it was me his eyes lit up, I knew he was happy. I handed him the plastic bag and I smiled, too, we were making our peace.

Kevin was asleep, dribbling on the pillow, still curled up in a ball, his little fists tight and his wet noonoo by his cheek. Well, there was someone who was happy, it made you feel good just seeing him. And envious. I slid in beside him, his feet were freezing but I could feel the warmth from his breath, it smelt good.

You took ages! Stan said in a sad little voice. I closed my eyes and rolled myself into a ball, too. Shit! always whinging, always questions, after doing the shopping surely I had a right to a bit of rest, my crying fit had worn me out, sleep would sort that out, why did Stan never take a nap? Lie down, I said, you need to gather your strength, I've got a surprise for you two. Really? he said, a bit suspicious, what is it? Lie down! I ordered… I mean, really! I was the mum, I was the one who should say what we did and when we did it, why wouldn't the kid lie down? Are we going home? I heard. I opened my eyes to look at Stan but it was so dark in the room I couldn't see him properly, I couldn't seem to understand why he'd said that. All these years I'd regretted my kids had never had a holiday and now we were here they could only think of one thing: getting home. They were cats, these kids, mustn't make changes. Never mind. I was glad, I really was, to have slipped my moorings, glad to be somewhere different, hardly any light, we'd got to the edge of the world and that was a good thing.

I sat up in bed and said to Stan, Listen, when I say a surprise I mean a surprise, okay? So eat some biscuits, trust me and let me rest. But what *is* the surprise? My God, he's made up his mind to drive me mad with his questions, any other kid would have jumped for joy if his mum told him she had a surprise for tonight, any other kid would have gone to bed to make the time pass faster, but mine was a mix of anxiety and suspicions, mine only took shallow little breaths, mine didn't trust anything or anyone! His teeth were chattering, I grabbed him by the shoulder. Lie down, I said, and I was so angry he obeyed me right away.

That's how I should have spent the rest of my days, in bed with my kids, we could have watched the world the way you watch telly: from a distance, without getting dirty, holding on to the remote, we'd have switched the world off as soon as it fucked up.

I rubbed Stan's back through the blankets to stop him shivering, for him to go back to being nine years old and let go of all those fears that don't belong to a child his age. I walked round the town, you know, I told him quietly, I've got the hang of it, we won't get lost any more, the man in the shop was all thankyous taking the coins, and this evening we're going to spend the rest, all the rest, that's all I'm going to tell you! I'd like to go home, he said very gently, he was begging me. I stopped warming him up, I lost interest in him, turned the other way and closed my eyes.

Yet again it didn't do any good. That room meant nothing to me, I was just passing through, between two strangers, it was a waiting room, a whispering gallery, there was a crowd around us, from before and from afterwards, which had left traces that were all muddled up. What was I, in the middle of all of them? What was I doing? I closed my eyes, and wasn't welcome anywhere any more, I was ejected, thrown out like some nasty little scrap. It was spinning inside my head, jostling about, I know that feeling well, it's what happens before the terrible thoughts, the ones that take me straight to the place I mustn't go, feelings I never have when I'm awake, yes, there are some things I can only do when I'm asleep, I go back to them in my sleep, that's where we've arranged to meet.

I buried my head in the pillow to make it go away, but it just thumped harder. It was knotted and heavy. Animals with pincers, scuttling little crabs who want to suck my blood. And they always tell me things aren't going well, things aren't going well at all, it's all gone wrong and it can still get worse, something terrifying's waiting for me and it's all my fault, I went about it all wrong and it's too late now. I try to fight it, to wake up a voice to say it's not true, nothing's going to come and gobble me up, I haven't made such serious mistakes, it was just kids' stuff, pranks that didn't mean anything, it was meant for a laugh, I do what I can, I'm not some giant, some perfect mother who lets everything roll like water off a duck's back, without leaving any scars – I know there are some people who are never hurt, shame I'll never be like them, I'll have to come to terms with that. I wasn't getting anywhere, there was no peace for me in that bed and I may well have slept the night before, but it was bound to be the last time, now something was holding my head above the waterline of sleep, I just had to realize it, that was all.

I opened my eyes, the room was almost completely dark now, you could hear rain against the window panes, the wind was up, if I'd been alone with Kevin it would have been easier, but there was Stan rebelling against everything, standing up to me. I looked at him as best I could, I wanted to know why nothing was straightforward with him, he'd started quietly eating the biscuits, nibbling at them, and he gave me a fake smile full of crumbs.

The sea must have been black now, too, like this shrunken patch of sky. The sea was swollen with dead sailors thrown into its waters, Hushaby. The sea was a freezing great floating graveyard. Was Kevin's enchanted castle still on the beach? Had the tide risen that far and snapped it up in one mouthful? And what about all those shells... other children will pick them up, when the water's all blue and the sun's broken through the sky. There'll be classrooms full of them, dead seashells, sick notes picked up along the beaches.

The rain was spattering against our window, poison released from above, the rain was at war with us, that's what was blurring the colour of the sky, would there be lots of lights at the funfair and lots of people, too? Here at the hotel you couldn't hear anyone any more. It wasn't a hotel, it was a tower, a rocket that never took off, we were closer to the sky than the others, suspended in thin air, with clouds pressing against the window panes.

Would you really like to go home? Is it because you miss school? That's what I wanted to ask Stan but the rain stopped me talking, lashing at the windows with its needles, I mustn't pay it too much attention, I knew that, had to think of something else, but was Stan really missing school? All day long with the teacher, how does that work? She bamboozles him for hours on end, telling him more and more stories! I can't even get him to read through his homework, I don't understand it at all, specially the maths, Forget it, he told me the other day when he realized I couldn't go through his geometry with him, is it really all that important? Calculating the angles of things? That's not how I see life, all flat on minutely squared paper, no more mysteries anywhere, school is the kingdom of numbers, even my kids measure them, weigh them, write them down, gauge them, they compare their average with the class average, why not with the national average while they're at it? That's the problem: we bring babies into the world and the world adopts them. We're the incubators, that's all, then they get away from us and it's not long before someone tells us we're no longer in on the act. Do I remember school? Do I remember being nine years old? I've forgotten everything. Apart from my father's songs, I don't remember anything. The psychiatrist at the health centre tries to dig up my memories, but nothing ever surfaces, nothing good or bad, nothing. I remember so clearly the sailor's shoes and the bed with the river flowing through it, but where my father was when he sang that to me, or my mother, my sisters, my brother – I couldn't tell you. It's lost. Fallen into a hole. You struggle to live as best you can but soon the whole lot disappears. We get up in the morning, but that morning doesn't actually exist any more than the night before which everyone's already forgotten. We're all walking on the edge of a precipice, I've known that for a long time. One step forward, one step in the void. Over and over again. Going where? No one knows. No one gives a stuff.

The rain was hurling its gobs of saliva against the window, tiny transparent flecks of spit, why were we being spat on? I didn't know but I was convinced if I opened the window I'd soon be filthy from head to toe. Was the wall opposite covered in it, too? Were the windows below getting the same as us? Were we all sheltering from this spit from the sky? I didn't want to know, nope, didn't care, no, mustn't think about it, never had thought of it, no, no and no again!

Are they good? I asked Stan. He didn't answer. He's gone off somewhere, he's good at that, Stan, slipping his moorings – oh, he's mine alright. The teacher lends him books and it's the same when he reads: he leaves us. Sometimes I think he carries on reading his books when he's given them back, he still thinks about them, he can read them even without the words, he's really very good at being somewhere else.

I let him drift and turned back to the wall to try and forget that the rain had it in for me. I looked at the brown paint, some black marks, holes in the plaster, patches of mould, but the fear had decided not to let go of me, I would have liked someone to ask me for something – anything, a song, a silly face – someone to make me talk out loud, someone to see me. There were things written on that wall, too, but you couldn't see them. I was like Stan, I could see in the dark, reading in a vacuum. It said on the wall that we weren't the first people in that room, that lots of people had been through there, hours of rain and no light, people who didn't know if outside was full up or just a void, who didn't know if we're too alone or there are too many of us, people who'd made love in this bed, lovingly or not, who'd fought too, thumping each other, lovingly or not, who'd said stupid things to each other, terrible things, the truth, and then lied to save themselves, to be believed... that bed up against that wall, that bed as big as the room, as small as it, that bed – what a piece of shit!

I could hear the rain smacking away behind me, and Stan nibbling, his new little teeth on the biscuits. Are they good, Stan? I asked more loudly, I'd like to have talked about them, to have wasted a bit of time talking about biscuits and Is it nice eating in bed, and Do you like the hotel and Do you think the rain falls straight out of the sky or comes swirling up from the middle of the earth? Yes, does it go upwards or does it fall? Does it spin round or fall flat? Stan! I begged him, are those fucking biscuits any good? I turned round and saw that Stan was talking to me, in the half-light I could see that he was looking at me and his lips were moving... I couldn't hear a thing, he looked worried, I threw the sheets back and got up. I left the room, the door banged hard against the bed, I ran to the bathroom and I stuck my head under the cold tap, to save myself. It was freezing. It hurt. It got inside my skull, I was being pulled by my hair, pulled towards the ceiling, my whole back was trapped in the ice, I was in pain, real pain, the explainable, logical sort, I was in brilliant white light, I was nowhere, in fact. I'd stopped falling. I got up. I woke up. I was breathing heavily from fighting the cold water, I'd made up my mind to win, to suffer for as long as possible, it felt terrible and wonderful at the same time, looking the enemy in the face at last, knowing exactly what's hurting, and emerging dazed, breathless, worn out. I was whimpering, the struggle was almost over, I was a solid mass of pain, it was coming to an end. I turned off the water. My hair hung down around my face, viscous little black threads. I stood up, then bent double as my spine gave way and the room reeled around me. When I opened my eyes I saw that both my kids were watching me.

Kevin threw himself at me, his head against my stomach and his arms round my waist, he tried to squeeze but he's got so little strength I could hardly feel him. Stan didn't say anything. How long was it since I'd taken Stan in my arms? I couldn't say. I'm taking you to the fair, I said. My voice was wrong, I didn't want to say it like that, in a whisper, I'd like to have said it all loud and happy, the kids didn't react. I took a deep breath and tried to shout, I'm taking you to the fair! but it came out faded and tired... the boys didn't move. Mind you, I'd have sworn they'd have followed me to the ends of the earth, but I realized the three of us didn't need to talk to each other any more. We could do things. Anything. The weirdest, craziest things. But without talking. We followed each other instinctively. We were sure of ourselves, like animals who never question, who just know what you should do and what you shouldn't.

We went back to the room and got ready. They got ready, choosing sweaters for the fair, trousers for the fair and even socks. No one would see them, it was too dark, but they felt smart. The evening was beginning. I just dried my hair a bit but the towel was very damp... anyway, what with the rain... drenched outside, drenched

inside, what was the difference? They did their hair looking at themselves in the window, You can see yourself in
the dark! said Kevin, Yeah! Stan said in a gangster voice,
better watch out, Kevin, you're twice as strong in the
dark! I made the bed so that it would be warm when we
got back, I went through the motions, the same ones we
go through at home. We put our wet jackets back on,
nothing seemed to dry them, they weren't waterproofs,
they were sponges, just putting them on was like going
out into the cold.

The stairs prepared us for being outside, too, and for
being seen. But there was no one there. On each floor we
thought we might come across someone, be surprised,
be their neighbour, but not a soul, not a trace, nothing.
I do think I heard a noise on the fourth floor. Something
falling, breaking. That was all. Six floors of brown, of
fire exits, banisters, silence and, downstairs, the smell
of sausages. Still no one in the foyer.

The rain had eased up outside, floating in little wafts,
the air was wet, there wasn't really anything coming
out of the sky, not properly, it was like the clouds had
come down to earth and were dying of boredom. The
ground was soaking, puddles all over the place, we
slipped on tyre tracks and other people's footprints as
if we were all trampling on each other, never in sync,
no one actually being the first to put their feet in any
one place.

The boys took my hands and at almost exactly the
same time the street lights came on: we were royalty. I

thought about the bus coming again and people getting off, like yesterday, visitors arriving in this damp town every evening, but to do what? Yes, people arrive here every evening and no one knows why, no one gives a stuff, they come, they go, it doesn't bother anyone, doesn't make anyone happy either, it's just movement, a bit of noise, no surprises, nothing to worry about.

I knew how to get to the funfair. You had to head out of town, towards the main road, that's what the man said. Fairs are often next to a main road, so the music doesn't disturb anyone. It's like with prisons, or nursing homes, anything that doesn't fit in with the surroundings happens near main roads, where laws aren't the same and pain is different.

I soon knew I was heading in the right direction: I saw sparkling lights driving back the darkness, and I could hear music. There, that's the fair. The boys still didn't ask any questions, they walked in silence, I felt they trusted me, they believed in me, yes, they believed in me completely.

We were gradually surrounded by people. Couples, groups of teenagers, I couldn't see any children... what was the time? Hard to believe it's exactly the same time for everyone at the same moment, hard to believe we have such important things in common. People were talking very loudly. They were digging each other in the ribs, they were joshing each other and laughing, pretending to be annoyed, the boys were pinching the girls and the girls had high heels and lipstick, I never looked like them, even at their age, and anyway I never was their age.

We weren't very far from it now, we could hear the music really loud but couldn't understand it, couldn't make out what the singer was saying, what he was bawling about, yes, it seemed a sad sort of song. The lights carved into the sky, threw up little fireworks, it was really strange to think we were going to step into that light, and take on a bit of colour.

People were running round us, overtaking us, they looked happy, were they the same people you came across in broad daylight? Was this a surprise for them, too, or did they always live like this, with a funfair next to the main road? I didn't recognize them, I wouldn't have dared pull faces at them behind their backs, they were so happy, they seemed strong.

What surprised me as soon as we got there was the smell. A reek of cooking oil and sugar, a smell that couldn't get lost in the crowd and followed everyone everywhere. It smelt greasy and everything seemed more dense than normal: the smells but also the lights, the music, the shouts, the laughter… no, you could hardly recognize these people, you'd have thought it was everyone's birthday, a day made specially for them.

I looked at my boys, they were wide-eyed, impressed, yes, they were impressed. It warmed my heart. I was proud. Obviously, we didn't feel at home there like the others, but that would come. We were feeling our way, carefully, like getting into cold water, only worse but we'd get used to it. The others were fine! They must be the same people who laugh and have fun by the sea when it's all blue, they like being together because they're all the same, or maybe not: they like being the same to be together... what I mean is it was difficult telling them apart.

If it wasn't for the mud I'm sure they would have danced, but it clung to everyone's shoes, it climbed up their legs, it churned with greasy bits of paper and spent firecrackers. With that mud you couldn't forget where you were, in a little town beside the rain, shoe-horned between the sea and the main road.

I knew what I wanted. I wanted to buy the kids some chips. Eating with your fingers was something Kevin and Stan really loved, and eating chips is always a treat. I looked for the truck. We went past shooting ranges and fairground rides, the boys looked but didn't ask for anything, taking it in through their eyes, maybe they thought we were only going to look, but oh no! we were going to do what the others were doing, it wouldn't be long, I was sure of it!

I found the chip stall. Chips. Waffles and candy-floss. There was a queue. We waited. Kevin had that cheeky little expression on his face, and when he saw me looking at him he rubbed his tummy, he looked happy. Stan was looking at a tall bloke in front of us, standing there with his hands in his pockets and chewing gum, and every now and then he'd kiss his girlfriend. But he always went on chewing his gum afterwards. Stan looked amazed, but the girl seemed to be used to it, she didn't find it funny.

The truck was making a terrible noise, its battery working flat out, it was hard to hear the love song playing on the sound system, the song didn't go with the lights, well, I didn't think it did, because the lights were flashing away trying to be cheerful and the song was going on about this poor woman who desperately wanted to dance with some man, like she was a seventeen-year-old but apparently she was much older and the man wasn't at all interested in her. I knew that song, I really liked it, they often played it on the radio. Take me dancing in the park, cheek to cheek in the dark... It was my turn, I ordered two paper cones of chips. I couldn't care less if the man whinged about my coppers, It was one of the rides, I said, that's what they gave me as change, didn't they? They've done me proud, haven't they? I involved him like that, on purpose, so he'd take the money and let me go. My kids were happy. Both of them at once.

We set off again, going right and then left, in the crowd, with the children eating their chips, and so I didn't lose them I held on to their hoods, like I'd dragged them out of a pool of water. We wandered aimlessly, there were people everywhere, the girls talking really loud, hanging on to each other or on to their boyfriends' arms, but always holding someone, always noisy and excited. The stallholders talked into mikes, It's starting now! Roll up! Roll up! And we're off! And bells rang overhead for the slowcoaches. I wondered whether in the end these people were actually happy or just in a hurry. Everyone was rushing around and it was because of all this rush that a girl knocked into Kevin and made him drop his cone of chips. He started crying. I didn't want that. I didn't want tears here, I didn't want anything to happen, just for us to walk about in all that racket that's all. I couldn't explain that to the poor kid because I didn't feel like shouting to make myself heard, so I carried on walking, holding him by his hood.

Stan had realized that the fair was for them, too, that they could join in, get excited, have a good shout, have their share of fun. He wanted to go on the dodgems. I said yes and paid. The cashier took the coins without really looking at them and gave me a token. The kids stood on the edge, enjoying themselves already, in anticipation. Kevin kept wiping his nose on his sleeve, but he looked relaxed now. I sat down on a wet bench a little way away, I'll wait for you here, I said, and their enjoyment vanished, they insisted I watched them. Hurry up then, I said, the session's over, and they rushed out towards the cars, incredible how children always want you to watch them.

I don't know how long it went on. The lights mingled with the sound system, becoming as depressing as the songs, you couldn't see the rain but it was following us all, it felt at home, it wrote things too, but I couldn't read them, the bells wouldn't stop ringing, people were hurrying onto rides in every direction, where did all that money come from, everyone could afford everything, there was too much of everything everywhere, too much noise, too much rain, too many lights, all reeling past me and I didn't know where I was any more.

Every now and then the kids would come and take more money from me and head back, they always asked if I'd seen them, I didn't answer. They headed off again. I waited in all that bustle, that turmoil, that rushing, trying to find a quiet corner to lay my eyes, I was the only person not moving, and then eventually I found it: up in the sky there was a big wheel full of whoops and screams, I settled on that and didn't let go. The people hung in the air for a moment then they were brought back down very fast – like in life. A breath of air and then you fall.

In the white lights of the big wheel the sky looked pale, I knew it was dark all around, nothing but darkness in every direction. And silence. I was in a furious pinpoint, with darkness all around, I was a star, old and always there, old and full of fire. I'd been thrown up into the sky, I wasn't holding on to anything but everything around me hung on, like I was cradled by arms.

I stayed there sitting on that bench and when we had no money left the kids came and sat down next to me. I was still looking at the big wheel. I liked hearing the people scream, they weren't real screams, nothing terrible was happening, it was wonderful. I was up there, in the white light, head down, feet in the air, I could puke up, scream with cold or joy or anger, I could do anything I wanted, I'd paid with golden coins, and down below the earth had turned upside down, a pathetic little lump, the crowd wasn't worth anything, milling about pointlessly, birds on a dung heap.

Kevin started snivelling, I came down to look at him, he said he was tired. I went straight back up again. I could see the sea from up there, it had reached a foreign country, all the fish had gone with it, and the seaweed, and the shells, all that was left were the rocks. I wrapped myself up in the darkness, followed the motion of the wheel, it was moving for me, no need to choose a direction, you just had to let yourself go, I was still in its arms.

Kevin started sobbing and Stan pleaded with me, How do I get back down to earth? I wondered, it felt so good in this volcano spitting flashes of light, don't feel like letting go and falling into the freezing cold mud, churned up by everyone's shoes, spread thick on the ground, no really, don't feel like landing in that mess.

Stan stood himself in front of me, I couldn't see the white light any more, I came back down in freefall, my head spinning while my body stayed still, Stan was shouting that we had to go back and go to bed, that Kevin was tired, that Kevin had been sick, that Kevin was crying, that Kevin was coughing, Stan was blocking the big wheel from view, with his wet hair and his huge mouth, I hardly recognized him. I looked over at the littl'un, he was sobbing, his shoulders shuddering, snot running from his nose over his mouth, and his legs kicking at thin air. The fun was over.

The cold had accumulated inside me without my realizing and it spread right through me when I stood up. My hair made my neck wet, icy droplets ran down my back, the rain always wins in the end if you don't watch it, the rain never forgets anyone.

I took Kevin by the hand and we left that funfair, going against the tide, in the opposite direction to the crowd, as usual. My back was stiff, I'd have liked it to be broken and then put back in place, I couldn't feel my feet any more, I was walking with planks at the ends of my legs.

We'd hardly left the funfair before we were plunged back into darkness, we could still hear the music and the screams in the distance, and the bells ringing, and the Roll up! Roll up! but it wasn't for us any longer, it was forgotten. No one will remember my little boys in their dodgem. What was the time? Still evening? Night time already? And the morning, when was that? Who was it for?

We walked on in silence in the dark, and the rain came with us while the funfair disappeared behind us, along with the girls who still had age on their side and the men hanging on to their arms, everything was getting smaller, their lives buried in the darkness. Where are those people when they aren't at the funfair? Maybe the girls sold shoes and the men were mechanics or delivered pizzas? Maybe they only laughed at the fair and the rest of the time they were just getting ready for it? Getting ready for that, I mean, for the fair. So their men didn't mind draining fuel from old cars, they knew that at the funfair they'd be the strongest, the proudest, ready to fight if they had to. Soon they'd be telling everyone about it, talking about it in cafés, hitching up their balls in their trousers, it's called memories. Me, I haven't got any. Everything that's happened is lost.

Kevin was lagging, pulling at my shoulder and snivelling, he didn't have any memories either, the fair was already forgotten, Did you like the dodgems? I asked him. What? he said in his sulky little voice. We went in the red one three times, said Stan, did you see us? There was too much hope in Stan's voice, I preferred not to answer.

We reached the hotel. I was frightened. We went into that place like going into a church. I often go into churches, when they're empty of course. There's a smell which makes you think about time passing, there are candles, there's silence, it always has an effect on me, a hollow feeling inside. Churches are very old but they are still standing. They are old but they never die. An empty church is something you can't explain, I like it. The hotel was the same. Something had to happen there. We went in with our rain and our mud, all that stuff we lugged with us, everything we'd picked up outside, we left traces of it all over the place again, the nightwatchman still didn't give a damn, there was another match on the tiny black-and-white TV, and what if it was always the same one? Always the same match on the same TV and us coming in every evening from that filthy weather and never hearing the nightwatchman say Good evening, how are you? Good night, madam, and what are the names of these two fine lads? He gave us the key, recognizing us without looking up, he knew his job by heart. I would have liked to ask him what time it was, what day it was, to have something clarified, the beginnings of an explanation about what was happening. He wouldn't have heard me. It wasn't worth it.

We climbed the six floors without holding hands, without talking, without complaining, Kevin wasn't even crying any more, he looked dazed, walking with great wide eyes, a sleepwalker. Those six floors were a punishment, it had to be done, all three of us had got the message there. I looked at my boys, sad, tired and struggling, it was the law, that's what I thought, These stairs are the law. Fuck this life where stairs are the law.

We didn't make a sound. We walked like old men, the ones who don't talk any more because they've got the message, so they just keep their heads down. Yes, we'd grown old. Let's hope it's not too late, I thought.

On and on we climbed, our place was up at the top, above the others, they were all asleep beneath our footsteps, and we climbed on. The nightwatchman's TV was just a tiny crackling sound now, the keys behind him hung there like bats and he didn't even feel the threat. We were breaking away from the earth, leaving a little bit of it on each stair, that was the mark left by my children, patches of dirt on brown lino. Their shoes had had it.

Eaten away by the sea, ruined by the rain, my boys were walking in exhausted old shoes, why should they carry on if even their shoes couldn't follow?

We didn't talk but we could hear each other. We could hear our breathing, getting louder and louder, were there people behind those doors to hear my kids suffering? Was their breathing getting inside their dreams, and blowing on them, snuffing them out? My God, I would have liked that so much, for my kids' breathing to have snuffed out all the dreams of people I don't know, and for there to be nothingness instead, a bit of room for nothing, behind every door.

We got to the sixth floor. There weren't any more stairs after that, we couldn't get it wrong. When it came to an end that was where we belonged. We knew that.

The room was freezing, the heating had gone off, I didn't have the strength to go and see the bloke downstairs. Last floor. Last leg. I wasn't going back down. I wouldn't complain, he could watch his match in peace. I felt the cold in there straight away, but I also noticed straight away that the room was lit by the moon. Not a beautiful round moon, no, but nearly a half, a roughly drawn shape but it shed a little light on the bed, there didn't have to be just rain in the sky, no, there could be something else, we'd moved on to something else.

Kevin wanted to go straight to bed. I didn't want him to. I wanted him to be clean. To have the face of a five-year-old, with no black stains from his tears and the rain, no snot or salt from his chips, no reminders of that day.

I dragged him to the bathroom and ran some water over his face, wiping away the stains and the hours, all those hours, I wiped everything away except his tiredness, but that... was for later. I gave him a farty kiss on his neck. He laughed. I did it again. He laughed again, a little laugh that couldn't cope any more, slightly irritable, slightly surprised too, normally farty kisses are on the stomach and on Sundays. But weren't we at home here? And seeing as we didn't know the time and seeing as we didn't know the day, we were free to do what we liked! But Stan came and joined us and told us to stop, we were making too much noise. There's no one here, I said, they're all at the fair, all out in the rain and we're never going to get soaked like that again, I'll never let that happen again, never, I swear to you. Your hair's still wet, he said, like I was a liar but at the same time I could tell he wanted to take care of me but couldn't seem to, he couldn't seem to any more. Have a wash and go to bed, I said and I took Kevin in my arms to cope with that big brown corridor.

How long was it since I'd carried a child in my arms? Billions of years. Kids grow up fast, they stick out in every direction, they're heavy, then you can only hold them by the hand but not hug them to you any more, otherwise you knock into each other, you don't know how to go about it, you get an arm or a shoulder in the way, you never find the right position. It isn't any better with babies. You're frightened you'll drop them, or make them sick, everyone says, Careful with his head! you have to hold the head, it's fragile, it's heavy, it can bump into things or tip back or twist the neck, it's dangerous holding a baby in your arms, it doesn't matter how often they show you how to in hospital, it's not reassuring, that's for sure. And when the head does stay put all on its own, the baby's not a baby any more and cuddles hurt. Maybe the only real cuddle is in your tummy, when you've still got the baby in your tummy, I mean. No one to tell you what to do, to say you're pampering it too much or not enough or not at the right time. You mustn't wake a baby. You mustn't ruin his appetite. You mustn't hurt his head. You're just with him. That's all. You're with him.

Kevin and Stanley were clean, they were ready for the night, as they said, yes, they often said I'm getting ready for the night, it's nice, getting yourself all sorted for the night, they never say I'm getting ready for the day, because daytime doesn't really warrant it, you've go to do it so you do, that's all, but at night there's a sort of preparation, like before a journey.

They got into bed, already accustomed to that brown hotel, the rain on the window, the false noonoo and even the cold, but I was afraid of the cold, I knew we had to fight it, that we should always head towards the warm not the cold, not into its world, its jaws, the sea of ice… like a glacier, what is a glacier exactly? Maybe we should have gone to see the sea of ice… were there buses to take you there? And beaches? And what colour was the water? White? Blue? Grey? A sea without waves, then, without noise, a sea that never stirred, never went away, was that it? Would Stan have been able to walk on it? Would it have made him happy?

It was too late now. Maybe we'd got the wrong bus and the wrong hotel, it was too late. They were here.

In the clean but old sheets. Don't sleep at the bottom of the bed, Kevin said, sleep with us. I promise, I said, but without meaning to, I broke the word in half, pro... mise, pro... mise, I coughed a bit, there was a huge lump blocking my throat. Quietly, very very quietly, I said I'm not going to bed yet, I'm staying here but not going to bed yet, okay? I'm watching the moon. But it was them I watched, I watched them go to sleep.

Kevin took a while, he was all wound up, his legs twitched all by themselves, making little kicking movements annoying his brother, but Stan was the first to get to sleep. Curled up, curled up so tight he looked like a little lump, a boy with no legs. If I'd had any voice instead of that knot blocking the way, if I'd had any voice I'd have sung a song to Kevin so he could sleep, too. But I was full of spiteful little aches and pains, biting away at me. My throat, my heart, my stomach and my hands were all wet. The rain had crept between my clothes and my skin, so that I'd never forget it, maybe it would leave scars, like an illness.

I could see the children's faces clearly thanks to the special night light provided by the moon. Kevin was looking at the wall, was he seeing the same things I saw earlier? Or was it a whole different story? What stories did Kevin tell himself to get to sleep – or to avoid getting to sleep? Sometimes he would say, I'm not going to sleep tonight, he was proud of that, but he never managed it and Stan would tease him. Kevin was like me, he wanted to know where we went to at night, where it took us.

He ran his finger over the wall, maybe he was inventing drawings, words, cuddles, or just nothing, maybe his finger was moving all on its own, maybe the rest, all the rest was going to sleep and his finger would go on... what was I going to do if a little bit of him never went to sleep? Is that sort of thing possible?

But his finger eventually slipped down the wall, and fell onto the bed, I heard the littl'un sucking his noonoo faster and he went to sleep. All of him. He was holding his noonoo against his mouth and his nose, all I could see now was his wet hair and his forehead... there were my boys... Both asleep and I didn't know where they were any more. In their dreams, each in his own dream, far away from me, somewhere else. With the moon overhead, wanting me to look at it, to look up, not down at the mud, the girls who sold shoes, the mechanics, the shopkeepers, the nightwatchmen and the men who served hot chocolate. Nothing down there could do us any harm now.

Why hadn't I watched the red car? Why hadn't I seen my two cowboys in their dodgem? Did they bump into lots of people? Were they the kings of the road? Were they brave enough to pay with my stupid bloody coins or did they get rid of them behind a truck, in a bin full of burst balloons and half-eaten bags of candyfloss? Had they lied to me? Did they already know how to pretend? Was it already too late?

The rain kept knocking on the window, insistent, wanting me to notice it, I couldn't give a stuff about it now, it was the moon I was looking at. The rain falls down, it's for all those people down below, I'm on the top floor. Higher up than the big wheel, higher than the sea, and anyway the sea had left town, it had got the picture long ago and pissed off, where the waves used to be there was nothing left but sand, with empty seashells, open ones, broken ones, not the sort you could give to anyone.

I remembered Kevin in the toilets at the café. Will you write a note? With mine, I knew the teachers corrected my spelling mistakes, Stan had been writing notes himself for ages, he just asked me to sign them. Stan knew loads of things already. Far too much. How did I end up here? There's childhood. Okay. Then straight afterwards there's the whole hostile world. You have to find that out. Had Stan already finished his childhood? I really hoped not. He acted grown up but he slept like a child with no legs, like he was still afraid and didn't want to take up too much room and get himself noticed.

They were sleeping differently now, with louder breathing, big sighs, it's the sighs that take the tiredness away, deliver us from it, a bit like tears, but can you cry in your sleep?

I'd decided to start with the littlest, start with Kevin, I knew it would help me for Stan, because without Kevin Stan couldn't be the big brother any more and that's who he was, yes, it was the littl'un first.

I lifted his head to pull out his pillow, it was damp from his hair, from his saliva and his noonoo, mustn't smell that pillow, must stay strong. I looked at the moon, that scrap of moon lighting Kevin's face from so far away, that light coming from so far away to my son's face. I sat down next to him, on the bed, with his knees against my back. I thought of those monks, there was bound to be one who'd just got up for me and he was a whole lot closer than the moon, he was just the other side of the door, a brown monk next to a brown door, with his candle in his hand and his never-ending prayer.

I put the pillow over Kevin's face and pushed down on it. With all my strength. I didn't want him to wake up and be frightened. I pushed even harder to make that chunk of time go by, the time for fear, because I know all about that and I didn't want to give it to him, I hope he never knew it, even when he waited for me at the school gates and I didn't come, not at the same time as the others, not when I was supposed to. I didn't want to spoil his face but I had to push hard and my shoulders hurt, I had to keep at it, for several minutes, to be sure.

My Kevin. We had some good laughs, the two of us. We had face-pulling competitions. Impersonations. Farty kisses. Jokes. Loads of things you're not supposed to do. My Kevin. I'd given him one wall in the house to do drawings, I called it Kevin's wall, he drew little men with no arms and red aliens, the social worker was horrified, she made a note of it in her book, but the littl'un loved that wall, when it was full up I'd paint it over in white and he started again.

I think it was six minutes, the exact time. You had to keep the pressure on for six minutes. I didn't have a watch. I looked at the moon and tried to feel the time passing, the raindrops kept on falling but they couldn't see my little boy any more, stupid bitches, he'd cried with cold, he'd kept his head down to walk through the mud and they'd bitten his neck, I hated them. Two days they'd been attacking him, with no let-up, and he was so defenceless, thinking the sea knew him and that you drink hot chocolate with a straw. My innocent boy, that pillow felt so heavy at arm's length, but it was taking everything far away, turning away all the bad luck, I had to hold on, hold on and think about you really hard, all my love on you, just for you, all of it.

I remembered the day Kevin wrote a word on the wall, his first word, it was me, it was mummy in stick letters, he was proud and so was I, that's who I was, he'd recognized it straight away, I was mummy, no more or less than the others, mummy, that's what I did, what I knew how to do, mummy, and I left it there, I never covered it with white paint so all the pictures had to be done round that word, MUMY, like the little stick men he drew, maybe I even saw their hands behind their backs while the red aliens spiralled round me, and I showed it to the social worker, my name on the wall in stick letters, how could she compete with that?

I was still pushing down on the pillow, Kevin hadn't moved, he was a good boy, he did as he was told. I was thinking only of him and I remembered his first word.

His first word came one morning when he was lying on the floor with loads of cushions round him because he couldn't sit up very well, he was blowing bubbles of spit, Stan was lying on the lino laughing, his head on his hands, really close to Kevin, and the littl'un leant forwards, he took a handful of his hair and said Stan. That was his first word. That evening in the kitchen Stan told me he wasn't his half-brother, he was his whole brother now, I said okay.

My arms hurt more and more, I changed them over from time to time pushing with one, then with the other so that they took turns to rest, but I was tiring faster and faster, I was hot, the raindrops on my back had dried and now it was drops of sweat that I could feel running under my arms. I could feel them breaking out and running down. One after the other. They went right down to my stomach. I mustn't think about it. I had to think about Kevin. All the time. All the time. Was he still dreaming? Was he already on his way somewhere else? Could he feel me? Was he alright? I looked at the white pillow, my wrist bent back, no strength in my hand, no blood, white against the white of the sheet, then a cloud passed over the moon and I couldn't see anything any more. How could I calculate the time? I could hear the rain on the window, how long did a song last, should I sing? No, mustn't leave Kevin, had to stay with him to the end.

I remembered the day I knew I was pregnant with Kevin. I was at the health centre with Stan, he had an ear infection, he'd cried all night, the neighbours had banged on the radiator, I was exhausted. We were in the waiting room, it was already Doctor Dart in those days – goodbye, Doctor Dart! – yes, it was always him who looked after the kids, and we were all jumbled up in that waiting room, old people, young people, tiny babies, there was coughing, there was shouting, you could hear children crying in the consulting room, it was hot, the phone wouldn't stop ringing, Stan was bright red and he was in so much pain he kept banging his head against the wall, whinging and banging his head, we waited a long time. I remember. No one looked at anyone else, except when a door opened because everyone was frightened of missing their turn, none of us liked being like that, jumbled in with the others, with their illnesses. I remember I was worried. I hadn't had my period for three months and I was often sick in the morning. And then a woman, an Arab woman, came and sat down opposite me. In her arms she had a tiny baby, I mean really tiny! Never seen such a tiny baby. And I knew I had one too. Almost invisible but secretly taking root. I nearly smacked Stan to shut him up. I got up and we left.

The cloud moved on past the moon and the glimmer of light came back. I thought I felt Kevin move underneath me but it was just my hand slipping. He was still motionless. Under the pillow. All limp. I thought that maybe he was dead but I didn't dare check. I didn't want to see him. Not yet. Was he blue? Were his eyes open?

Did he still have his noonoo in his mouth? Maybe the noonoo had helped him, maybe the noonoo had suffocated him too and I needn't have pressed for so long?

I remembered his father. Kevin often saw him without realizing it, and he didn't know either, the father. Well, he may have guessed, he might have wondered. I don't know and it's better that way. He was very young, he'd left school and was training to be a plumber, something like that, his parents were the caretakers of our building, he came to the flat once, something to do with exterminating rats, I think, or a Christmas box, I had a problem with my radiators and he came in to have a look. He reminded me of my brother, that boy, Didi they called him.

In the end, memories don't always help. It was like the things I was thinking about were taking me away from Kevin, I've always had trouble concentrating for any length of time, but who could tell me how much time had passed? I'm not used to memories, do they take long? Are they quick? How many times had I changed hands? Was I hurting Kevin? Was he frightened? Had the moon moved in the sky? Was it getting lighter and lighter or was it me getting used to the dark?

All of a sudden I was frightened Stan might be watching me, like he watches me when I stay sitting in the kitchen for hours. And I didn't even know where Kevin was now. Death is full of people, but where are they all? What are they like? And, most of all, how do they get on together? Stan really had to join Kevin, he couldn't be left all on his own like that, Keep an eye on your brother, Stan, keep an eye on your brother... I lifted the pillow. Very gently. Slowly. I lifted it high up above Kevin's head and then I put it down on the bed so I could see. See my little boy. He hadn't moved. His face was still turned towards the wall. His hair all over the place. His eyes closed. But his noonoo wasn't in his mouth any more. I realized it was over. I moved right up to him, he wasn't breathing any more, he didn't smell of him any more already, he wasn't sleeping any more, no, it was something else.

I stayed there, looking at him for a while. He was dead. I put his hands under the covers so they didn't get cold. The moon was making little pictures on him, shadows, little men just the way he likes them. I pushed the hair off his forehead, tidied it a bit and then I kissed him. You should always kiss the dead. My head was spinning, my mouth was full of cramps, full of ants, even the roof of my mouth and my teeth. I was thirsty.

Stan moved. It startled me. He turned his face towards me. I had to get on with it. Get on with it fast. Very gently, I picked the pillow back up, walked round the bed, on tiptoe, and sat down next to him. My back was blocking the moonlight. I couldn't see a thing. I would have liked to see Stan's face one last time. He was in the dark already. I couldn't tell what he was thinking, what he was dreaming, and did he already sense that his brother was dead? Kevin was waiting for him. He couldn't be left on his own at the gates of death, at just five, how would he cope? I had to work fast. I couldn't. I couldn't make my mind up, I'd already given so much for Kevin, it had taken so much effort to see it through, to remember and feel the time passing.

I wanted to open the window and feel the rain on me, have a good dousing and look right at the moon, if I could have landed on it like I did on the big wheel, rested a bit somewhere far away and full of light, if I could I would have done it, would have breathed that distant air.

I had one child dead and the other alive. That was no good. You can't have that: one here and the other on his own. I'd rather have both hands empty than have an arm missing and lean to one side like a cripple. I had one child dead and the other alive, I had to get a move on.

I was holding the pillow tight against my stomach and I rocked for a while to give me courage. I shouldn't have let Stan get so big, what was he thinking about on that beach, just before he thumped my arm? He had walked along that beach like he was used to it, had he seen it all already? Was it really too late? I'd let him grow up because he was the older brother and the littl'un couldn't go without him, one without the other was impossible, you have to appreciate that, one without the other... And before? Yes, before Kevin was born, what was Stan like? I couldn't remember... I can't picture myself in hospital, or walking in parks, I see myself standing over him at night, watching him in pain, when a baby coughs I always think it's going to tear itself in half, I was afraid of that, yes, I was afraid for him, definitely… but it's all so hazy, and maybe it isn't him, maybe I'm the one I can't capture any more because I wasn't really there.

What was the time? Do we go around the moon or does the moon go around us? Are there any people in this hotel or did I imagine someone knocking on the wall, someone dropping something, I don't think this hotel makes a profit, no, it should be demolished, and quickly too, rip off the doors and pictures, make the earth shake under those beds that are too big for the rooms. I prayed for the earth to shake, I said, Oh God make the earth shake! and I rocked myself with the pillow against my stomach.

Stan moved slightly, he turned his face towards the window, it made me jump, and what if he woke up and saw Kevin, how could I explain and convince him to go too? Stan was moving, but maybe he wasn't there any more than his brother was, he was wandering in a dream, the closest country to death. Yes, I had to take my chance while he was dreaming and then he would do like Kevin, he would simply slip from one country to the other.

I looked outside. It didn't look like morning was coming, at night the hours stretch out, all hooked onto each other, all the same, nothing to tell them apart, that's why it's so long and that's why you can get lost in it. Living those hours through the night one by one can drive you mad, it's like having an eye ripped out, you lose your balance… and that badly drawn moon which couldn't make up its mind to be a proper one was no longer helping me now that my back was blocking its light. It wasn't generous and dazzling now, I'd thought it was on my side but deep down I knew everything had given up on me. I had to take care of Stan, who would give me the strength?

He moved again, his hands came out from under the covers, I was sure his cheek had creases from the pillow, but I couldn't see well enough to check. He had such fine skin and the sheets always left marks on him. He used to grumble about it. When I got up it was already too late, they'd faded, but he told me about them, he often told me it worried him, I'd never seen it, this thing that bothered him.

I looked at him for a long time, like I wanted to get inside him, to find a little door and be inside him, he once told me how come we stand on the ground instead of falling over or flying away, It's because the earth pulls us towards it, he told me, and I wanted it to be the same here, to be pulled in by him, for him to be my earth, and definitely, definitely not to hover above him but fall towards him like a magnet.

And I put the pillow over his face. I covered it and then sat closer, right next to his face so I wouldn't let him go, not ever. And it was him, it was Stan who helped me. He didn't struggle, just his legs a bit, straightening out in little jerks, he tapped my back, and I liked it, how long was it since our bodies had touched each other, just our hands, nothing else for such a long time, since for ever perhaps.

His legs stretched out and then he went quiet. Kevin had pulled his hair and said Stan and he said He's my whole brother and there was the day he picked him up from nursery and the littl'un was all upset but full of admiration He's my whole brother and the day Stan threw himself in front of a barking dog to protect him He's my whole brother and the breakfasts Stan used to bring me in bed on Sundays the sound of the mug against the plate Kevin's little footsteps following him a whole family and Stan watching me sleeping and Stan watching me stare at the kitchen wall and Stan who's afraid I'll wake up on my own a whole family a family far away from the hostile world.

I was exhausted. My hair had fallen across my eyes, drenched with rain and sweat, were they together at last, did I have to go on struggling, my heart was pounding, there was only one heart now for three people or was Stan still there? Who was on their own? Kevin or me?

Never cold again, I thought. And I pressed. Never cold or ashamed again. My arms were so tired they were shaking, I turned my face to the moon, it looked so bloody proud, up there, so high up there, asking me whether I could hold out for a whole night, one whole night isn't so hard, I'd held on for so many years, with the chemicals, without the chemicals, with sleep and with insomnia, with my own kids and with kids that the world swallowed up.

I collapsed, my body against Stan's. Between our two faces, a pillow with his last breath in it, my son's last effort. I got back up gently, I was sweating and cold. I took the pillow away, put my face very close to Stan's and I saw it, I saw the mark left by the sheets on his cheek. He hadn't lied. I kissed him, there, right on the mark, his soft crumpled skin.

I had two dead children. And them? What did they have? I stood up to look at them both, now they were the same. I looked at their bodies hidden by those old sheets and thin blankets, Kevin's curled up in a ball and Stan's stretched out. I looked at them and I saw. I saw something I'd never thought of, something I'd never imagined ever: Kevin's face was turned towards the wall, and Stan's towards the window. They had their backs to each other. They weren't together, no, each had gone his separate way. They weren't joined together in death, they'd lost each other there.

And I screamed.

# Subscribe

Subscribe to Peirene's series of books and receive three world-class contemporary European novellas throughout the year, delivered directly to your doorstep. You will also benefit from 40% members' discount and priority booking for two people on all Peirene events.

PEIRENE'S GIFT SUBSCRIPTION
Surprise a loved one with a gift subscription. Their first book will arrive tied with a beautiful Peirene ribbon and a card with your greetings.

The perfect way for book lovers to collect all the Peirene titles.

> 'What a pleasure to receive my surprise parcel from Peirene every four months. I trust Meike to have sourced for me the most original and interesting European literature that might otherwise have escaped my attention. I love the format and look forward to having a large collection of these beautiful books. A real treat!' GERALDINE D'AMICO, DIRECTOR, JEWISH BOOK WEEK

Annual Subscription Rates
(3 books, free p&p, 40% discount on Peirene events for two people)
UK £25   EUROPE £31   REST OF WORLD £34

Peirene Press, 17 Cheverton Road, London N19 3BB
T 020 7686 1941
E subscriptions@peirenepress.com

www.peirenepress.com/shop
with secure online ordering facility

# Peirene's Series

Peirene curates its books according to themes. Each year we publish a new series – three books which form a cluster in terms of style and/or content. All our authors are award-winners and bestsellers in their own country.

........

## FEMALE VOICE: INNER REALITIES

...........

## MALE DILEMMA: QUESTS FOR INTIMACY

Free Peirene e-book samples can be downloaded at:
www.peirenepress.com/samples

*Peirene*

# Contemporary European Literature. Thought provoking, well designed, short.

'*Two-hour books to be devoured in a single sitting: literary cinema for those fatigued by film.*' TLS

---

Online Bookshop

Subscriptions

Literary Salons

Reading Guides

Publisher's Blog

# www.peirenepress.com

Follow us on twitter and Facebook @PeirenePress
Peirene Press is building a community of passionate readers.
We love to hear your comments and ideas.
Please email the publisher at: meike.ziervogel@peirenepress.com

# Peirene Press is proud to support the Maya Centre.

The Maya Centre

*counselling for women*

The Maya Centre provides free psychodynamic counselling and group psychotherapy for women on low incomes in London. The counselling is offered in many different languages, including Arabic, Turkish and Portuguese. The centre also undertakes educational work on women's mental health issues.

By buying this book you help the Maya Centre to continue their pioneering services.
Peirene Press will donate 50p from the sale of this book to the Maya Centre.

www.mayacentre.org.uk